FINAL DELIVERY

FINAL DELIVERY

AND EIGHT OTHERS

MARK THORSON

atmosphere press

CONTENTS

The Dope Runner

3

The Fifty Dollar Assassin

17

Malfunction Junction

37

A Trip Back Down

59

The Gift

73

Last Stop At The Stop 'N Go

123

Stranger's Day

129

A Good Piece Is Hard To Find

159

Final Delivery

169

To Liz Cava, whose loyalty and support in the early years
made this book ultimately possible.

Expect trouble as an inevitable part of life.
Ann Landers

THE DOPE RUNNER

Jack knew he had made a mistake.

But didn't know where.

He had been very careful about the whole thing—he had done everything right. From the *pick-up* in Arizona to the *drop-off* in St. Paul—he had carried out everything flawlessly.

That's why he had taken the job. Because he was good at things like this. He was smart. He was also in great shape—and not bad with guns either.

The money was good too. Six grand a trip.

But the money wasn't the reason he had originally gotten involved—he had always had *cash*. He had gotten involved out of *depression*—after his longtime girlfriend had dumped him for a thirty-five-year-old GQ stockbroker downtown. The dumping had put Jack into a serious funk—a painfully ugly doldrum—where nothing seemed to make sense anymore, where nothing seemed to matter—including his own life—which left him somewhat defiant and somewhat open for a little adventure.

But after his first run now, all of that was beginning to change. He had been suddenly feeling good about himself again—feeling confident and optimistic. In fact, for the first time in his life he felt like he was accomplishing something on his very own—something out of his own merit and skill—rather than just accepting something he'd been given, like a trust fund, or his college tuition, or a summer job at one of his dad's Twin Cities car dealerships.

Just the way he had run the package out of the southwest desert—out of the San Simon wash—had been a significant accomplishment. He had shoulder-strapped and belt-cinched the pack firmly to himself, then had run, trotted, and climbed for seven hours straight, moving through darkness and over rugged terrain, then had jogged on, in treacherous heat—through snakes and cactus and over uneven footing. When he finally reached his Trans Am, he had motored up Highway 82 into Phoenix—doing so perfectly, without drawing a speck of attention—then up to Flagstaff, where he cleaned up at an old hotel in the downtown area. He picked out a room on the corner of the top floor, which was a perfect lookout, and a great site for a shootout—had the situation come up. The room had reminded Jack of the one Steve McQueen had in *The Getaway,* except the one Jack had was even better.

Yeah, Jack had certainly been careful alright—and ready for anything. He had thought it all out beforehand—and had equipped himself accordingly. In his Trans Am he carried a

9-millimeter Smith & Wesson with a fifteen shot staggered clip—carried it in a quick-release holster just ahead of him, underneath the dash. It was a stainless steel model, just like the ones the guys in that movie *Pulp Fiction* used, except Jack knew how to handle one, and the guys in the movies *didn't*. Jack had been handling guns since his early boyhood—firearms of all varieties: shotguns, rifles, pistols—the works. He knew everything there was to know about them too: he knew loads, projectiles, actions, riflings—and he could hit a target too—*moving*. On his person, he carried a fourteen shot .380 Berretta, which he kept in a modulated holster attached to the inside of his jean jacket—which was another thing you never saw in the movies. Those guys—movie guys, like Mel Gibson or Stallone or Schwarzenegger—they were always carrying some big oversized hand-cannon—like a .45 or .44, or some big, bulked-up .357 pig, which, the second you fired it, would box your ears in so damn bad, it would just about knock you silly. In reality, while the movie guy would be trying to get his bearings back, anybody with half a wit and a smaller, quicker .380, could easily let fly with another three or four rounds—and accurately too.

But these sorts of things were just common sense, and they were also the reason why the movies pissed Jack off. You had retreads writing the goddamn things and you had morons watching them.

Which, generally, all boiled down to one thing: *People were stupid.*

From Flagstaff, Jack had headed east on I-40 towards Albuquerque, and then north up to Santa Fe. He drove the speed limit and used his turn signals and thought about that shootout back at the hotel. He thought about the shootout in

5

The Getaway some more too—and also about the one at the OK Corral. He thought about assault rifles and politicians and movie people, and about the public in general—how goddamn dumb they were.

Take assault rifles for an example—which Jack contemplated as he cruised up I-25 towards Santa Fe. Everybody was so damn afraid of the things. "Scary," everyone liked to say. But not many of the "scary" crowd were concerned about shotguns, which were a hell of a lot more accessible and far more deadly. A plugless short-barreled .12 gauge had a lot more firepower—at least at close range—than any AR-15 or AK-47 did. It was just common sense. Simple ballistics. An old hacked-off 870 Remington would clean out a room full of Hollywood movie guys with assault guns any day. Assault rifles, as they called them, were for Army guys. In other words, dumb ghetto kids and ignorant farm boys who thought that the guns looked "neat," and would easily pick one up and go off to die in some war that they knew nothing about.

Or take the OK Corral as a case in point. A classic shootout with .12 gauge shotguns. If a person could go back in time, back to the old West, and take away the Clanton's shotguns and give them assault rifles instead, they would've gotten their asses kicked even worse.

Again, it all came down to the same thing: *Public stupidity.*

Alongside Jack, in the seatliner on the passenger side of the Trans Am—built into the rear of the backrest—Jack kept a sawed off pumpgun loaded up with number two buck.

Yeah, he had certainly been ready alright. Armed to the teeth. He had enough firepower to launch a small scale war, and he had been prepared to do it too—if necessary. Well, not really—but if he had to, he could've.

From Santa Fe, Jack continued north towards Denver—checking his rearview for approaching cars and watching the open country for anything that wasn't right. He glanced up through the tinted sky panels, checking for airplanes and choppers, and did all of his gassing up in rural areas—at Exxons and Stucky's out on the interstates—out in the middle of nowhere—where he could see who was coming, see what was approaching. He never let the Trans Am out of his sight, and he never wandered off into wayside rests. He never entered any restaurants, and he was ready at all times to *pull down* on anybody that got too close—too close to his *load*.

As Jack passed through Colorado Springs, he had felt an urge to stop for a couple of beers, but had quickly thrown the idea out. He had decided to play it straight. Play it smart, be professional. Drink mineral water, take vitamins, and eat healthy food: vegetarian.

But he had really wanted to stop, and it was a terrible shame that he couldn't have, because he was at his peak—really looking prime. He probably could've picked up any chick he had wanted to. His hair was cut short, specifically for the job, trying to pass as an all-American jock—which wasn't too tough to do, because that's exactly what he had been just a few years before. He had a good tan to go with it too—and he was in great shape, like never before. He had a twenty-nine-inch waist and a forty-two-inch chest, sixteen inch biceps, and good quads and calves too. Yeah he was looking good alright—and most chicks, if they could've seen him, and *seen what he was actually doing*—would've been absolutely knocked right out. The only exceptions would've been a few of the Buick Regal types whose lifelong goal was to marry their way into the suburbs, where they could park their asses in front of a television set, wear the latest hair, and shovel their faces full of a bunch of high fat, fiberless garbage.

But any real chick, any *babe*... would've been absolutely blown right over.

Somewhere north of Denver, Jack hit the wall and had to pull off the interstate to get some rest. He pulled into an approach off a gravel road and nosed the Trans Am back outwards again for a quick getaway. He shut the engine off and sat in darkness for a while, and then just looked and listened. That had been an exceptionally peaceful part of the trip. When he finally felt confident that he was alone and not being tailed, he laid his seat rest back, gripped his 9-millimeter Smith under his jean jacket, and went to sleep.

But by the time dawn arrived, Jack was already back on the interstate, headed out across Nebraska on I-80 where he started to dream about having a shootout with Federal Marshals and ATF guys, which, by the time he hit Omaha, was a hell of a scene. He had dead SWAT guys lying out in the corn, wearing those silly black ninja outfits, and FBI agents wearing those foolish cop-show windbreakers lying strewn out along the highway—several of them *women* who had wanted so badly to be a cop, had wanted so badly to be a man.

After Omaha, Jack entered Iowa, and after Des Moines he headed north on I-35, and it was about that time that he started to think about the *drop-off* up in the Twin Cities. He had checked out the address before he had left, finding a nondescript cinderblock building in the industrial district, located near the river in South St. Paul. Jack had been given a key, and had been instructed to enter the side door at exactly two o'clock P.M. on the date of his arrival, and then to sit down in the black chair at the center of the room.

And then to just wait.

Which is exactly what he did.

The chair sat out in the middle of a large open area on a cement floor—facing two other chairs with a small table in between—which was where Jack had been instructed to set the package...

Which he did.

The place had natural sunlight glowing in through overhead panels and clear-cubed blocks on the upper walls. Jack sat in the chair and listened to the sounds of a construction yard somewhere down the street. He examined the rows of pallets and pails stacked along the walls and looked at the package on the table in front of him, which he had kept exactly the way he had received it—in a tightly bundled Gore-tex backpack.

It was somewhere around this time that Jack began to feel uneasy... uneasy for a reason he didn't quite understand. He was nervous. Even scared. He couldn't rationalize it, so he decided that it was just instinct—which in turn, bothered him even more.

Maybe it was just the idea of getting busted, he thought. He began to think about the moral and ethical aspects of what he was doing—which led him to thinking about the Kennedys—about old Joe making all that money running liquor during prohibition, which, to Jack, damn near justified his own actions. No, better yet, it gave the whole thing a very American dynamic. Even made it somewhat respectable.

But none of this seemed to help Jack's nerves.

Jack decided that this would be his last run. He would go for a couple of beers afterwards, then go home and get some rest. Maybe in the morning he would even go see his dad, and take his old job back. His dad would be thoroughly impressed with Jack's new appearance. The shoulder length hair that had so severely disgusted him was now gone—and he was clean shaven too. He looked like a young Republican, which was exactly what his dad had wanted—had wanted so badly, had wanted for so long.

Suddenly a sound—the abrupt *jarring* of a door, which turned Jack around in his chair. Two men had entered the warehouse from the rear, and were walking towards him. One looked like an all-star wrestler with a tight orange t-shirt; the other looked like a convict—a seasoned, weathered convict—older and smaller, but meaner.

Jack turned forward again. Did so on instinct. Don't look, don't stare. And don't make any eye contact. Just stay calm, stay cool, and get through this thing.

Jack suddenly wanted out. His heart had started to pound.

Two more people were sitting down in the chairs across from Jack—and Jack hadn't even seen where they had come from. It was a man and a woman—the woman Asian, elegantly dressed—but it was the man that gave Jack the creeps. He was about forty-five, with tight oily skin and black eyes that didn't blink. He wore yellow slacks and a red golf shirt, gold bracelets, and big rings. He looked like a shark in country club attire. The man was dark, but he wasn't black. He wasn't Cuban or Mexican either. Jack didn't know what the hell he was, he just knew that the guy wasn't from the suburbs, and that *he,* Jack, wanted out.

Jack suddenly felt like he was in a cave with a pack of wolves. The Asian woman sat at an angle on the chair next to the shark, her legs crossed, facing the shark but looking past him to the wall off to the side. She wore an expensive evening dress with golden earrings and flashy bracelets. She looked like she was on her way to a formal affair somewhere, her hair tied perfectly back in a stylish bun. She pulled out a cigarette from a golden case with a green dragon or seahorse on the side and lit it. She never looked at Jack. She looked only at the pallets and pails along the wall, smoked her cigarette, and spoke to the shark—speaking towards his ear, in a tone that Jack could not hear.

The shark looked directly at Jack and asked him questions. Short, direct questions. *Did he talk to anyone? Anybody touch the package?* Did *he* touch the package?

Jack nodded and shook his head and answered, "no" and "no" and *"no,"* in a voice that was higher than his own. The shark's eyes made repeated contact with the two thugs behind Jack—which kept Jack's heart pounding wildly in his chest.

Then the convict stepped forward and took the pack off the table. He opened it up and checked the contents, and as he did this, stepped back behind Jack again. The shark did not speak anymore. He just stared at Jack.

The place was quiet. Exceptionally quiet. The only sound was the light business of the convict inspecting the backpack, and Jack's own heart thumping uncontrollably in his chest, which was now climbing up into his throat, taking the breath out of him. When he opened his mouth to get air, it made an audible *clucking* sound, Jack was sure of it.

At this point, Jack told the shark that he could keep the money—that he really didn't want it—which, next, Jack thought was probably a mistake, as it could possibly be interpreted by the shark as an admission of guilt. The shark just held his eyes on Jack. The woman smoked her cigarette and stared at the pails.

Jack knew at this point that the predicament was not good. He thought about offering the guy his car too—which, before thinking any further, he *did*.

Then Jack noticed the black eyes shift to the two men behind him again, and the next thing Jack knew, the two thugs had hold of his arms and were pressing them forcefully downwards onto the armrests of his chair—one on each forearm, pinning them down with enormous force.

It was at this point that Jack knew he had made a mistake.

But Jack did not struggle. Again, it was instinct. Maybe it was the embarrassment of struggling and losing in front of a woman. Maybe it was the thought that if he didn't resist, that then maybe—just maybe—he would be treated with more mercy.

Which, perhaps, was another mistake.

By the time Jack noticed the syringe in his arm, the contents had been mostly dispensed. The convict had stuck it into Jack's lower forearm, just above his wrist—which was another thing Jack had never seen before—had never seen in the movies—which again, for a fleeting moment, kind of pissed him off. In the movies they were always sticking needles into the *upper* forearm. But this was the *wrist*. And this stuff was *real!*—and again, *the goddamn movies had gotten it wrong!*

The syringe dropped to the cement floor, and the two

thugs continued to hold Jack's arms.

Then the dark man and the Asian woman stood up and started away.

Jack thought about a short story he had read a long time ago—back in junior high school—about a man being hanged on a bridge during the Civil War, who, when the trap door opened beneath him, imagined the rope snapping loose—and himself then falling to the river below, where he swam ashore amidst heavy gunfire and then escaped into the woods—after which, when he was finally in the clear, found that his fantasy had ended, and that the rope above his head was just cinching taut and snapping his neck.

Jack thought about his own fate. He thought about being burned in his car. He thought about being dropped off out in the middle of Lake Superior—of being sunk into the depths, never to be found, to be forever preserved in the frigid darkness with the missing crew of the *Edmund Fitzgerald.* He thought about all the life he had wasted. Just goddamn *wasted.* Watching bad television, showing off, trying to impress people he didn't even like. He wanted nothing more now than to just *walk*—than to just *breathe,* than to just *think.* He thought about his ex-girlfriend and the stockbroker downtown. He thought about a girl he had known in school—Sheryl Kruehns—and wondered where she was, what she was doing. She was deaf—and spoke in a funny monotone voice—but she was very beautiful, and Jack had always liked her. Jack had often thought about Sheryl Kruehns, but had never let anyone know about that—including her.

But right now, for some crazy reason, Jack wanted to be with her. He wanted to be with Sheryl Kruehns like nothing more in the whole world— and he wished that he could at least let her know about that.

Jack tried to concentrate, tried to focus. He tried to stay straight— tried to fight the drug—just as he had done so many times in the past— trying to sober up after getting drunk, after getting the spins... He saw a fleeting image of his dog—his best friend from his boyhood—his dog Kipper. Jack had held Kipper while the vet slipped a needle into her fur and put her to sleep. It was the day before Jack had left for college—left for Arizona State.

Jack thought about his mother and wished that he could go home to see her, and maybe bring Sheryl Kruehns...

Jack was sorry for everything he'd ever done. He thought about God, and asked him for mercy. Not for help, but for mercy—to clear his name, to make right for all the wrongs that he may have committed. He had never wanted to hurt anyone. He had never intended to hurt anybody—and now he hoped that he never had.

He also hoped that his mother would not find out... He hoped she would never know about the places he had been... or about the things he had done... He hoped he hadn't disappointed her... He hoped that... He hoped... tha...

***

Victor Bull picked up the empty syringe and slipped it into his pocket.

He took hold of the boy's body and lowered it from the black chair down to the cement floor, then carefully stretched him out onto his back.

From his rear pocket, Victor pulled out a thick flap of

bills held together by a single rubber band. He counted quickly through them with his tattooed thumb. Sixty of them. Then he reached down into the boy's inner jean jacket and felt around for an inside pocket, finding a holstered weapon—which he left undisturbed. He thought for a moment, then folded the bills over and stuffed them into the boy's front jeans pocket, where they would be easily noticed upon waking, easily found.

Victor Bull then stood upright again and glanced about for anything left undone. When satisfied, he walked away from the boy, crossing the warehouse floor to the door at the rear of the building, which he then stepped through, and pulled firmly closed behind him.

THE FIFTY DOLLAR ASSASSIN

Summer 1988

"Fifty dollars?"

The Assassin nodded.

The Professor glanced over his shoulder and around the bar, then lowered his voice a bit further. "And that includes everything, right? I mean checking it out, killing him, getting rid of him—everything. For fifty dollars. I mean, I just want to be sure about this."

"Fifty bucks and he's gone," said the Assassin. He didn't lower his voice at all—just took another drink of beer. He was drinking Grain Belt from a bottle.

The Professor and the Assassin were seated in a booth at the Hay Creek Tavern, engaged in a contractual discussion that would result in a killing. The tavern was located twenty-two miles north of town—just off the Reservation line—along a gravel road in pine and swamp country—*Indian country*. It was a place for lumberjacks, trappers and thieves, for renegades and alcoholics off the Reservation, and for people that broke down out in the country who were desperate. The place had a buckshot-riddled beer sign over its front door and a small dirt lot that sparkled with broken glass when the sun managed to catch it through the trees. Inside, it was dark and unclean, filled with a mild funk of dead game and body odor—of stale beer, hamburgers and vomit—most of which was spiked with a steady strain of cigarette smoke and a variety of jukebox music that ranged from Travis Tritt to AC/DC.

"May I ask how you'll do it?" said the Professor. "I mean, I assume it'll be at night, and I imagine you'll use some sort of a silencer or something."

The Professor received only a deadpan stare as a response, to which he took a quick sip of beer himself. Then he said, "I think the Fourth of July would be a good time. I mean, not right on the Fourth, necessarily, but you know, on that weekend perhaps. I'm just thinking of all the fireworks and noise, and all the activity and so on."

The Professor received only more of the same stare, to which he quickly added: "I just don't want you to get caught."

"Caught?" said the Assassin. He offered a brief smile, to which the Professor was momentarily taken aback—mostly by the high quality of the Assassin's dental work.

None of this was working out like the Professor had expected. The Assassin himself, for example, was nothing like what the Professor had imagined him to be. He was... *different*. And he was *certainly different* than that of his contemporaries at the Hay Creek Tavern, who were a roughshod variety of physical and mental absurdity. The Assassin was not a large person, but was built strong and authoritatively. He wore a faded Levis jean jacket with colorful beadwork along the collar and shoulders; his hair was long, straight and rebellious, his features distinct and handsome. But there was something else, something just beneath this ethnic armor—something that set him apart from the others, which caused the Professor to conclude, that for an Indian, the Assassin seemed very... well, *white*.

"I should maybe just stay out of it," said the Professor. "Except for giving you some money, of course. This sort of thing just isn't... well let's just say that it's not exactly my area."

"What *is* your area?" asked the Assassin.

"Excuse me? Oh... teaching. And study."

"Teaching what?"

The Professor looked at the Assassin again and reached for his beer. "Ah... Ethics."

"Ethics?"

The Professor nodded with raised eyebrows and took another sip. Then he added, "It's essentially a dissection, or a view—or I should say, a reasoning, or an explanation of various human behaviors. At least that's the form that I teach."

The Professor looked away to avert the Assassin's stare again, and as he did, took another swallow of beer. He was drinking Grain Belt from a bottle, same as the Assassin— knowing that it was *Indian beer* but trying to be a Roman while in Rome. The Professor tried to recall the last time he'd drank the stuff—and as he did, watched a slobbering man in the corner—*an Indian*—struggling to get another swallow of the product. It probably hadn't been since he was a kid, he thought—seventeen or eighteen, back in North St. Paul—back when beer was beer, and the only issue of interest was price and alcohol content. It wasn't until later, when he became of age that he became conscientious of the social distinctions associated with beer—learning that Grain Belt was *Indian beer*—that Old Milwaukee was construction workers beer—that jocks drank Miller, Pabst and Bud—and that old men who were out of touch drank Hamms.

And of course that people of *culture*—intellectuals and *academics*—drank imports. The Professor's fridge at home contained Heineken and St. Pauli Girl.

"You know that guy?"

"What?" said the Professor. "Oh, no. No, I'm just... I'm sorry, you'll have to excuse me, but I have a bit of a fascination—actually it's an ingrained respect—for the Native American culture."

"He's an Indian."

"What?" said the Professor. He blinked, then smiled and cleared his throat. "I was just referring to your culture, to Native Am—"

"It's *Indian,*" said the Assassin. "Chippewa Indian."

The Professor looked blankly at the Assassin, beer suspended, mouth open.

"I imagine you dislike Columbus too."

"Columbus?" said the Professor. He set his beer down and adjusted his glasses. "I'm sorry, but I don't quite see what—"

"I don't care if you can see or not," said the Assassin. "Just don't use that reference anymore. At least around me."

"Sure," said the Professor. He put his palms up in defense of himself, feeling a warm rush of blood swell up onto his back. "That's not a problem. Not at all. That's fine."

THE PROFESSOR

His problem started not long after the ink was dry on his new mortgage—which was for a six figure home that his new wife, who was younger by eighteen years, had picked out along the lake.

She had been a student of his at Hamline University in St. Paul, and after they were married, the Professor had suggested that they move up north, to live on a romantic lake in the woods. His idea was to escape the scandal and controversy of their relationship at Hamline, and to provide her with a better, more grandiose existence than he could afford her in the city. He also considered her vibrant youth and explicit beauty and decided that the ratio of male competition would be greatly reduced in a smaller, more rural setting—a setting that was perhaps, *less educated*. Also, he would be a big fish in a small pond up there, rather than vice versa. He would teach at a small state college, and she could spend her time reading and becoming literate as he had been planning for her to.

But what the Professor actually ended up with, was not exactly what he'd had in mind. Instead of a quaint, *Waldenesque* hideaway in the forest, the house turned out to be a luxuriously over-sized layout in a neighborhood full of *Republicans*—a group the Professor had spent much of his life trying to avoid, both socially and academically— and one which his new young wife was quickly befriending and finding to be the *absolutely most wonderful people.*

There was also the dog.

The *dog:* a big, wild, unwanted thing that also seemed to come with the mortgage—appearing on the Professors front lawn shortly after the purchase was finalized at the bank. The animal was enormously large—part German Shepard, part Timber Wolf, according to the neighbors—and a definite menace. The creature began spending its time— nearly all of it—on or around the property—chewing on the shrubbery, digging in the flowers, lifting its leg on the front steps—as well as on the garbage can, the lawn mower, on the side of the house, on everything.

According to the neighbors, the wolfdog belonged to a trailer house full of people who lived down the road and back in the woods. *Bad news welfare cases,* they told the Professor—and the Professor had been warned, and thoroughly advised, to avoid them at all costs.

Using this information, the Professor decided to deal with the animal himself, directly. He tried simple verbal dissuasion at first, followed by mothballs...

Then he tried a slingshot.

But the slingshot infuriated the animal and turned it hostile. So the Professor decided to up-grade his firepower. He decided to try an air-pump pellet gun offered to him by the dentist, who lived two houses down, just next to Bud, the highway contractor. The Professor hoped that the *zing* of the air gun would overwhelm the animal, and permanently discourage it from any further interest in the area.

But the stinging little pellets turned the wolfdog meaner. *Viciously meaner.* And soon the animal dug in, and began to counter-attack. It chased the Professor across his yard, and snarled wickedly at him, flashing its yellow teeth.

The Professor gave up the air gun—and other methods of dissuasion—but the wolfdog did not give up its new-found hatred. The dog also took up ownership of the Professor's large front steps— claiming them as his own—where he would bark ferociously at the Professor and often block him from entering his own home.

The Professor sank further into the depths of despair. He became consumed by a hopeless state of depression and frustration.

Then he heard a voice.

It spoke to him *from above* one afternoon while he was sneaking around the side of his house trying to re-enter through a back window—a precaution he had been taking for several weeks. The Professor looked up to find a man on the roof—dressed in white—the house painter the Professor's wife had hired to do the shutters and eaves. The painter suggested to the Professor that he get rid of that big dog.

"I've been trying!" said the Professor. He shielded his eyes and squinted up into the sun. "God knows I've been trying, but nothing seems to work! And there are no ordinances or municipal laws around this place—it's like living in the wild west!"

"If you want," said the painter, "I know a guy who'll take care of that sucker for ya."

The Professor asked, *Who,* and the painter told him, *Eddie Thunder.*

"*Who?*"

"The hockey player."

"*Hockey?*"

"Yeah, you know, the Indian! The *Boston Bruins?*"

The painter told the Professor that Eddie Thunder was

back on the Reservation and that he was sometimes available for, *'shit like this.'*

"A couple weeks ago I seen him take out a whole pack of 'em at Bass Lake," said the painter. "There was a bunch of dogs—wild scraggly lookin' bastards—all runnin' through the yards and wreckin' stuff and raisin' all sorts of hell. So this guy hired Eddie to come out and take care of it! *Fifty bucks a head!*"

The painter broke into a wide grin and looked off in the direction of the lake. "I was paintin' a house down there along the south end and here come ol' Eddie, pulls up right alongside the pack in an old Buick, steps out with a pump shotgun and cleaned out the whole works—all in about five seconds! It was the funniest goddamn thing I ever saw in my life! He had dogs layin' all over the place!"

The Professor was taken aback by the barbarity of the painter's story. He told the painter that he could not agree to such violence—that there had to be a more civil, more sensible way of dealing with the problem.

"Suit yourself," said the painter. He ran an arm across his forehead, then held his brush towards the Professor again. "But for fifty bucks you'll get rid of that ugly mutt. And if you stick around... you'll also get a hell of a show!"

THE ASSASSIN

During his youth, they jammed arenas to see him play, and when he signed with the Boston Bruins—and then resigned as captain of the team—posters and calendars of him went up onto bedroom walls—not only on and off the Reservation—but all across the country.

But then came a disagreement between Eddie Thunder

and coaching staff member, Dick Baird—which resulted in Eddie telling Dick one day that he was going for a beer, to which he then walked out the doors of the Boston Gardens and never went back.

There had been one of those changes in the wind that Eddie's grandmother had always told him about—and had taught him to respect. She had taught him that these changes had little to do with the manners or customs of others, but had everything to do with his own *spirit.*

Eddie had experienced this as a boy—after he had left the Reservation to play in town—and then experienced it again after graduation, when he turned down offers to play in the NHL—the NFL and in Major League Baseball—and took the full ride hockey scholarship at Yale instead.

He had experienced it again when he left Boston, and was experiencing it now, back on the Reservation, where he spent most his time in the woods—hunting ducks and deer and trapping fur.

During the summers he also fished the lake and raised marijuana in the swamps—selling most everything he caught, shot, or harvested on the black-market, mostly to restaurant wholesalers and black-market bootleggers from Minneapolis-St. Paul. The fish were mostly walleye pike; the ducks: mallards, bluebills, and teal. The fur were red fox, beaver, and muskrat—the meat of which also went to restaurateurs in the Twin Cities—mostly to the *take-out* type, of the Chinese, Thai, and Vietnamese variety. The marijuana was raised amongst a rogue stand of birch, near a cedar swamp, where Eddie planted and harvested by the moon and sold to a small handful of dealers in ten pound bales—who in turn, bagged it and sold it to individual peddlers as *Columbian* or *Maui Wow-ee*—who in turn, sold it to college kids, mostly northern white kids who understood nothing about the plant, and thought it to be the best dope in the country.

The deer he did differently.

During the winter months he hunted for people on the Reservation who were too old, poor, or disabled to get enough meat for themselves, and in the fall—during the season—he hunted for hire, selling mostly to hunters from the Twin Cities who had come up north to bag the great *whitetail deer*, but who had failed. He sold the deer for whatever he could get—fifty dollars usually, sometimes more for bucks—a hundred, two hundred— sometimes as much as five or six, depending on the size of the rack and the desperation of the hunter. The hunters would then strap their purchases onto their cars or four-wheel drives and parade them the two hundred and fifty miles back home, showing off their kill along the way, and impressing their wives, girlfriends, and their small circles of friends once they arrived—showing off proudly the ferocious animal they had bagged while in the dangerous wilds of northern Minnesota.

The most lucrative sale he ever made was a fourteen-point trophy buck that he had sold for eighteen hundred dollars to a fat corporate tycoon in a shiny Cadillac. The tycoon was heavily weighted with gold chains and diamond rings, and every time he said something that Eddie did not like—which was every time he opened his mouth—Eddie raised the price another fifty dollars, until finally, the tycoon shut himself up and made the purchase at eighteen hundred. Eddie imagined the deer's head to be mounted in the fat man's estate in one of the wealthy suburbs of Minneapolis—probably Edina, or Wayzata, or somewhere around the Lake Minnetonka area. It would be a fine conversation piece during dinner parties—as a tuxedo-clad orchestra performed soft music and women in long evening dresses sipped wine. The men would stand about in clusters of importance, holding their drinks in front of themselves, discussing issues of manliness—like money. Then, at the appropriate time, when enough inquiries had been made, the fat corporate tycoon would gather the guests around his enormous trophy and tell the story of how the ferocious animal had leveled its rack of antlers and charged him— telling of how he had stood steadfast in the path of the deadly assault, emptying his rifle into the vicious beast until it was nearly upon him, and how he had then fired his final round into the big buck's neck, dropping it to its fate only inches from his own feet, and only inches from his own very probable death.

Yes, it would be stories like these. They gained men such as this an illusion of power and respect—and their women probably treated them well in bed after such heroic tales.

But that was for men such as this. Not for men such as Eddie Thunder.

Any respect for him was now gone.

It was lost.

After Eddie Thunder walked off the ice in Boston and away from his three million dollar contract, the posters and calendars came down. People back home, in town, reacted to the news variously—some without apparent surprise— some saying that they always knew something like this would happen one day, that *it was bound to happen,* because Eddie Thunder was an *Indian,* and that this sort of thing was just the *Indian* in him.

Regardless, Eddie Thunder was no longer recognized as the individual he had once been. He was no longer the idol of people's children, no longer the pride of the community. Those who had once called him a hero, a star, a *great one,* now called him a loser, a poacher, a drug dealer, a no-good Indian.

But to Eddie Thunder, these were merely people who had numbed themselves into believing that they understood life. They were people of an establishment that raised ill children and blamed their deficiencies on things such as dope or alcohol, or on T.V., or guns, or on the devil, or politics, or music, or on anything and everything except for themselves. They were a people who had been blinded by the light of their own recklessness and deafened by the noise of their own machine. They were a people who had been seduced by glitz and flash, and hypnotized by *show,* and they were unwilling—or unable— to accept the harder and truer realities of life. They were a people who judged *him* to be unethical and inhumane—to be a savage killer—while they thought of themselves to be decent and civilized— hiring others to do their killing for them, the results of which were collected in a neat cellophane wrapper, paid for over a counter to a smiling young girl at a checkout register.

Yes, Eddie Thunder knew these people. He had played their games and followed their roads—and knew that neither of them led to any place of any significance or fulfillment. He had gained their knowledge and accomplished their methods—and for leaving their path, he was now recognized as a problem. At best, he was seen by some as a confused figment of myth, legend, and lore; but by most, he was now seen as little more than a *no-good Indian... as* a recluse... as just another renegade off the Red Lake Indian Reservation.

THE ASSASSINATION

The Fourth of July was a beautiful day—perfect for the picnic the Professor and his wife had planned for the neighbors and their families. Picnic tables, lawn chairs, and barbecue grills had been set about on the lawn, down by the lake, and the turnout was a grand success. Bud—the highway contractor—and his family, had been the first to arrive, then came the banker and his family, and then the dentist and his. The lake was at a natural calm, without a stitch of wind, and it was busy with swimmers, boaters, and water skiers. Kids splashed in the lake and dug in the sand as neighbors and friends socialized on the lawn and visited over chicken, drinks, and potato salad—at each of the quaintly arranged picnic tables. The only dismay was that the Assassin had not yet struck. The wolfdog was still at large—and present at the picnic—lying in the shade beneath a spruce tree, eating another piece of chicken that he'd helped himself to off one of the barbecue grills. The ranting and heckling from the kids and neighbors had not—as usual—persuaded the animal to leave.

The Professor, wearing a golf visor and clip-on sunglasses, paced the beach in frustration, chucking stones into the lake. He had become seriously disenchanted with his hired man, the Assassin. He had expected him to strike during the previous evening, while fireworks popped about the neighborhood and exploded over the lake, but there had been no such fortune. Having prepaid for the assassination while up at the Hay Creek Tavern, the Professor was now considering the possibility that maybe—just maybe—he had been *taken.*

But it was as this thought was passing through the Professor's mind, that a deep rumbling tremor turned his attention towards the house—the sound of a bad muffler and rock 'n roll. As the Professor turned, glancing up the hill, he caught sight of an old car pulling into his driveway—a rusted-out Buick with all of its windows down—

Suddenly the Professor's heart skipped. It lurched up into his throat and began to pound. The Professor felt his knees go weak, felt his bowels loosen. He looked across at his new young wife—who stood barefoot out in the middle of the lawn, white cut-offs and tan legs. She was also turning and looking up the hill towards the new arrival— as were several of the neighbors.

The Professor immediately started towards the vehicle, but then stopped. He swallowed deeply and inhaled a gulp, trying to settle his pulse.

The car pulled to a stop and the engine died. The rock 'n roll stopped and the air fell quiet.

The Professor couldn't move. He stood where he was, like a statue, in shorts, visor, and clip-ons, looking helplessly up the hill—watching as the driver's door of the Buick opened up and Eddie Thunder stepped out... .

The Assassin just stood alongside the rusted car for a moment, looking vacantly towards the Professor's house. He took a drag off a small cigar, then looked at the group below, near the lake, and started towards them. He walked in a relaxed, authoritative manner—almost a saunter—like some sort of sauvé rock 'n roller...

The Professor didn't know what it was, but something about the Assassin looked strikingly different than it had up at the Hay Creek Tavern. Although his hair had been cut and groomed, he looked like *what*—like one of those characters the Professor's wife watched on MTV. He wore red polished cowboy boots—*expensive* looking boots—with faded blue jeans tucked inside, an open flapping trenchcoat that looked like something a U.S. senator might wear, and a bright yellow t-shirt underneath that looked like a freshly opened can of paint. He wore round wire-rimmed sunglasses with crimson blue lenses, one hand inside his coat pocket and the other pinching the small cigar.

As he descended the long sloping lawn towards the lakefront, a slow wall of plush, deep green rose up behind him and all remaining movement amongst the neighbors seemed to dwindle into stillness. Kids and parents stared—everybody did—as if some slick gunslinger was strolling into their saloon, stopping the piano player, the card games, the dancing girls, everything.

"Hi there Eddie," said Bud, the highway contractor.

"How ya doin', Bud," replied the Assassin.

"Happy Fourth, Ed," said the banker.

The Assassin nodded to the banker, then stopped in front of the others, making a brief scan over them with his crimson blue lenses—which ended on a beautiful young woman in white cut-offs who was just sitting down at the end of one of the picnic tables. The young woman looked at the Assassin, and for a moment everything seemed to fall silent again...

The sound of a motorboat hummed somewhere in the distance. A slow wave washed in on shore. The Professor started to say something, but then stopped himself and sat down along the edge of an adjacent table.

The Assassin took a final drag off his cigarillo, then dropped the butt to the grass and pressed it out with his red polished boot. He then turned from the young woman and looked across towards the barbecue grills.

"That him?"

"That's him," said Bud. "He's been a hell of a problem around here." Bud was seated in a lawn chair, wearing tennis shorts and drinking a Pabst Blue Ribbon beer.

The Professor's wife looked down at the Assassin's red polished boots and watched them as they started out again across the grass, walking towards the dog.

The wolfdog looked up at the Assassin from its place in the shade and started into a low growl.

"I wouldn't get too close there, Eddie," said Bud.

The wolfdog suddenly rose to its feet and growled *viciously* at the Assassin, it's face smeared with barbecue sauce. The Assassin, not breaking stride, pulled out from his trenchcoat a sawed-off shotgun—a .12 gauge pump with a sling.

"Oh my goodness," muttered one of the neighbors.

"Oh my God," said another.

The Assassin jacked the slide in a quick *chit-chit,* leveled the barrel and fired a *BOOM!* which threw the wolfdog back and around and onto the lawn—stunning the breath out of the picnic in a very audible, *"Ahhhh!!!"*

The Assassin ejected the spent cartridge with another quick *chit-chit,* then reached down and picked up the shell casing and slipped it into his pocket. Another slow wave washed in on shore. A boy on the beach said, *"Wow!"*

Another boy said, *"Cool."*

"Now that wasn't so bad was it, Professor?" said the Assassin. "Just a little mosquito bite."

The wolfdog lay on the lawn, its muzzle mouthing something inaudible, it's front paw swiping lifelessly at the air.

"Oh good God," said the Professor. He put his hands up over his face and turned away. "Oh good God, good God, *good God!*"

Bud, the highway contractor, squeezed at his jaw, and some of the neighbors moved physically closer to one another. The Professor's wife remained where she was, at her place at the picnic table, her eyes still on the Assassin. She had watched the spent cartridge pinwheel into the air as the Assassin had ejected it—watched it spin in a purplish, golden glint—then stared at it after it landed softly on the lawn. It was beautiful. A brilliant royal purple with a shiny golden powder cap.

"Anybody got a camera?" asked the Assassin.

One of the boys ran up from the beach—the one that had said, '*Cool.*' "I do!" shouted the boy.

"Grab it," said the Assassin, "and get a picture of this."

"Sure thing!" said the boy. He was about ten years old, in a swimming suit, sporting an oddly shaven haircut and a big grin. He reached across a picnic table, over a paper plate of watermelon rinds for a camera, then turned towards Eddie Thunder.

"I'll count to three and then you snap the picture, okay?"

"Sure thing!" said the boy. He took a position up close, planting his bare feet firmly on the lawn, in a half-crouched racing stance.

The Assassin leaned the pumpgun up against a birch

tree, then knelt down and lifted the wolfdog's bloodied head up alongside. "Okay, one... two—" then the Assassin reached into his trenchcoat and pulled from a shoulder holster a short barreled revolver—a silver plated .357 police Ruger—cocked it and stuck it up against the wolfdog's head. As he did this, the Professor noticed the Assassin's bare shoulder—noticed it as he flapped his coat back, exposing momentarily the tan muscular symmetry of it— and in that single instant, the Professor prayed to God that the Assassin would not, at any time before leaving, take the trenchcoat off, as he was terrified by what his wife's reaction might be. There was also something else that both overwhelmed and annoyed the Professor in this very same instant, and that was the parallax of both the barbarity and the pure artistic beauty of what was in front of him—how the Assassin's movement and the color around him was like physical poetry—the faded blue jeans kneeling on green grass, the open trenchcoat with the bright yellow t-shirt underneath, the crimson blue lenses, the tanned complexion and black hair, and even the silver gun— how elegant and expensive it looked, glinting in the sunlight like a fine piece of jewelry. The whole thing, as disgusting as it was, was just... well, as the painter had put it, *a hell of a show*.

"Three."

BOOM! The gun and the camera sounded simultaneously, although only the power of the gun was heard. Blood and brain matter blasted out the exit side of the dog's cranium and onto the grass, jolting the picnic again into another genuflection of turning heads and lifting hands. Some of the neighbors moved even closer to one another, some clutching their children tightly, others cupping their mouths.

Only the Professor's wife remained unmoved, still seated at her place at the picnic table, her eyes still on the Assassin...

The Assassin stood up again and looked out at a passing speed boat—a glossy red one pulling a teenage girl on a water ski.

The Professor expressed his disgust with the Assassin, and asked him to *leave. Immediately! Please! With the dog!*

The Assassin turned to the Professor and started towards him, holding the shiny revolver loosely at his side. The Professor took a single step backwards and swallowed deeply.

The Professor's wife looked downwards again and watched the red polished boots pace back across the lawn, moving past the Professor. She followed the boots until they stopped—which, when they did, stood directly before her...

The Assassin re-holstered his .357, then reached down and took the young woman's hand and placed in it the purple shell with the shiny golden powder cap. He looked into her eyes... and she looked at his, looking into the crimson blue lenses...

Bud, the highway contractor, took another drink of Pabst. The Professor readjusted his visor...

Then the Assassin turned away from the Professor's wife and walked back over to the dead wolfdog. He picked up his shotgun and slid the sling up onto his shoulder, then reached down with one strong hand and hoisted the carcass up over his other shoulder. *Chinese takeout.* Then he turned to the boy with the camera, and said: "Be sure the Professor gets a copy of that picture, will you? Tell him to take it to school for show and tell."

"Sure thing!" said the boy.

Then the Assassin turned and started up the long sloping lawn.

"Thanks Eddie," said Bud, the highway contractor.

"You bet, Bud," said the Assassin.

Nobody else spoke until the Assassin was nearly to his car. Some of the kids crouched around the scene of the killing and poked at the bloodied grass with sticks. A couple of the parents told them to keep away from it, to leave it alone. Neighbors looked at the grass and out at the lake. Some looked in the direction of the Assassin, but only in brief glances.

The Professor's wife did not move at all. She held the purple shell in her hand beneath the picnic table—where she caressed it with her fingers and squeezed it gently in her palm. Her eyes did not leave the Assassin. She watched him throw the dead animal into the back seat of the old Buick, then watched him get into the car, ignite the rumbling engine and re-start the rock n' roll.

Then she watched him drive away.

As others resumed their conversations and movement, the Professor's wife remained where she was, holding her gaze in the direction of the Assassin... where she continued to hold it, long after his car was gone... and long after the sound of his music had faded.

MALFUNCTION JUNCTION

November 1978

When it happened, they were headed for the Junction to get more beer and some shells for the new shotgun Chet Stoolberg won at the Ducks Unlimited Banquet. Chet was driving and Howard was on the passenger side, slouched down, drinking the last of the Schmidts. The pickup was fishtailing on the ice again, and Chet was letting off on the accelerator, steering side to side with it, trying to straighten it out.

"You drive like a pussy," said Howard.

Chet kept his eyes focused on the road. "Well, it's just a little bit slippery in case you haven't figured it out."

"Slippery," mocked Howard. "Shit, you're just a goddamn pussy." Howard sat relaxed during the side-swaying—sitting with his Sorel boot ankle resting over his knee. He was staring down at the November issue of

Sleaze Babe magazine—at the Babe of the Month sprawled across his lap in a tempting pose.

The Junction store was eight miles east of town and Chet and Howard were halfway in between. The Junction sold gas, beer and minnows, and other items of local necessity—of which Chet and Howard were planning to pick up another twelve pack of Schmidt and about six or eight boxes of shells, and then head north ten miles to Inquist's slough—a vast stretch of barren muskeg, brush and thickets—that ran north to the Canadian line. Howard had been slaughtering the Honkers and Blues up there for several weeks, and now the northern flights of Swans and Snows were coming down. He had been trying to get Chet to go with him all season long but Chet was always avoiding it—always complaining that Inquist's slough was too much work, *too much of a pain.*

Chet liked to hunt geese the easy way—the clean, easy way—either in the convenience of his own backyard or from the comfort of his new Ford pickup.

Chet touched his shoe back to the accelerator again and began creeping the pickup carefully back up over thirty. Howard's attention remained on the Babe of the Month—on her pale nude body, her tossed-back hair and parted lips, and on her eyes which were gazing up at his begging for it—*just begging for it...*

Howard took another gulp of Schmidt and glanced out to his right, at the slow passing land. It was late morning, almost noon, but the day was dark, the world a gunmetal grey. The drizzle from the previous evening had turned to freezing sleet during the night and then to snow, leaving the roads glazed over to a slick, icy glare. The land was lightly dusted with a fresh covering of white leaving the frozen fields blotched and patched, and the distant pines flocked bright with virgin frost. The whiteness seemed eerie in the air's murky darkness. It was a day in which the world seemed to remain asleep, as if lying down for the coming winter. It was a day in which people would remain indoors—in which women would bake and talk on the phone, and men would sleep in front of the TV, or would drink beer and watch Wide World Of Sports.

It was also a day in which driving was treacherous, and travel was done only by the desperate and by the foolish.

The back of the pickup had started to slide again, and again Chet let off on the accelerator, ruddering back and forth with the wheel, trying to straighten it out.

Howard said to him, "If you're gonna go in the ditch, at least wait 'til we get some more beer, will ya."

Chet didn't answer. His eyes were pinned to the road with the concentration of a surgeon. He had turned the radio off a couple miles back and hadn't touched his beer since they'd left town, leaving it resting on the seat between his thighs. They were riding in silence—the only ones on the road—the only sounds being the light blowing of the heater fan and the recurring *whiz* of the rear tires spinning-out beneath them.

Chet got the rig straightened out again and then slowly touched his shoe back to the pedal, creeping once again carefully back up to speed... 29... 30... 30... 31...

"Goddamn season's gonna be over before we ever get there," muttered Howard. He readjusted his slouch. Then he said, "Shit, I should've brought my sister along and let her drive."

Howard was restless—restless with Chet. Chet bugged him—or at least the way he handled things did. Chet was always so *neat* and *careful* about everything, and that really irritated Howard. Just like the shotgun he'd won at the DU Banquet—the one that was on the rack behind their heads—a brand new Remington 870 pump. The banquet had been almost eight weeks ago but Chet still hadn't fired it yet. And it wasn't that Chet hadn't been hunting. He'd shot plenty of ducks—and geese too—but all with his old Mossberg. He didn't want to use the new one because it was *too new*. That's right; *too new*

And *that* was just the way Chet had gotten to be. That was the new *Chet Stoolberg.*

And he'd gotten that way about *everything.* If you went out to his house—the new one he'd built on the lake—you always had to *take your shoes off*—and everything was always perfect—and you never dared to touch anything—and you never knew where to set your beer. Or like his pickup—the one they were riding in at the moment—a brand new, shiny blue Ford; it was always spotless, and it still smelled new, and Chet drove it like an old woman on a Sunday. He never carried anything in the back unless it was soft, because he didn't want to scratch the box, and there was never anything on the inside either—never anything on the dash—no gloves or screwdrivers, no shotgun shells, maps, tape measurers, or anything of the kind. The only thing ever to be found in Chet Stoolberg's cab was whatever he happened to get in with, which on this day—one of the last days of goose season—was their shotguns, their clothes, their beer, and the copy of *Sleaze Babe* magazine spread across Howard's lap.

Howard took another swallow of Schmidt and looked across at Chet again—watching him for a second—watching him try to drive. Chet was leaned forward over the wheel like he was going a million miles an hour or something—concentrating on the road like one of those senile old farmers that couldn't see. He looked stupid. Everything about him looked stupid— the way he was sitting, the way he was dressed—everything. He never dressed right anymore. Like today—for hunting geese: he was wearing jeans with a skinny cowboy belt, a bright yellow Hawaiian shirt with orange and purple swirls, and a red plaid, flat-topped, Scottish sport cap. On the seat between them laid his coat—a full length double-breasted trench coat with wide lapels. Add a scarf and goggles and he'd look like one of those *Magnificent Men In a Flying Machine.* In the back were his hip boots, which he was planning to slip on in place of his wing-tip dress shoes. That's right; *wing-tip dress shoes.* Howard tried to picture what Chet was going to look like shooting geese in Inquist's slough with all this stuff on at once. He'd look... what, part tourist, part poet, part gangster, or something. Howard wasn't exactly sure what he'd look like, all he knew was that it pissed him off.

"You look stupid as hell in that hat."

Chet kept his eyes on the road. "Well I'm sure the geese are really going to care." He said it slowly, as if one false syllable would send them into the ditch. "I'm sure they'll say, 'Hey, look at that stupid looking hunter in that hat. We're not going to land by him, we're going to go land by some official looking guy like Howard Dunvold who's got all the proper gear on.'"

"I don't give a shit what they say," said Howard. "You look dumber than a sonofabitch. You look like some sort of retard or somethin'."

Howard, on the other hand, in his own estimation, looked *great.* He had on his old weathered duck coat—damn near beige now—and his beat up camouflage hunting cap. He hadn't shaved in about four days, leaving a scraggly growth on his face—and he smelled right too. His coat and gloves had been marinated in several years' worth of game kill, leaving a wild odor to his gear of dead fowl, dried blood, and feathers.

But Chet... Chet was ridiculous.

And it wasn't just the way he dressed or drove anymore, it was the way he hunted too. His idea of hunting these days was to sprinkle bread crumbs along the shore in his backyard, down by the dock, and then go relax in his living room—and watch Donahue or something—while the ducks gathered down at the lake. Then he'd slip out the back door during a commercial with his old Mossberg—his bath robe still on—sneak up behind the wood pile while the ducks were eating and quacking, and then unload on them, nailing about six or ten at a crack. Then he'd go down and finish off the cripples, pick them all up, and usually be back in the house— just propping his feet back up with his slippers on again— before Donahue asked the next question.

This sort of thing really irked Howard; the whole approach did—it really rubbed him the wrong way. There was something terribly wrong with it, something unethical about it. The way it was supposed to be done, was the way they were going to do it today—*Howard's way, the traditional way*— by sneaking out into Inquist's slough, through the bog and snow, and then lying low in the thickets while the big flocks of Honkers and Snows moved in from above. Howard could just see it—Chet and himself, just like old times—waiting in stealth as the flocks lowered closer and closer and then began dropping onto the muskeg. He and Chet would spring up and open fire on them, blasting the living hell out of them, and then chase down the cripples—sloshing through the bog and thump-grass—and finish them off too! Then they'd drop down flat in an instant again—reloading in a scramble—as another flock circled overhead. They'd lay there still as death until that next flock began dropping in, then they'd spring to life again, blasting and pumping away at them too!

Yeah, that's the way they'd do it today—the *right way, the real way*—blasting away until their shoulders were sore and they had more goddamn geese than they knew what to do with. Then, at the end of the day, they'd head over to Howard's place to clean birds, and then, later on, head over to the *Power House* and tell all those suckers hanging out around the bar and pool tables about their big shoot—and lie like hell about it, about where they got them.

"Down the river," they'd tell them. "Way the hell down there—by Plum Lake!"

Plum Lake. Yeh, you bet.

Howard *loved* it. He loved the whole damn thing—the thirst for the kill, the take down, the body count, all of it. He took another swallow of Schmidt and looked out at the slow passing land again, riding with the pickup's gentle side-sway as if sitting in a drifting raft on a smooth flowing river. It was at this moment that he happened to think of all the *suckers* in the world—people who lived in cities, who sat in traffic jams and breathed shit air; people who couldn't do a damn thing because there was always somebody right next to them, right on their ass, bitching; people whose lives were *so* suckered, that their idea of *doing something* was paying admission to sit on their ass and *watch somebody else* do it.

Yeah, those were the suckers.

But not *them.* Not Howard Dunvold or Chet Stoolberg. No sir, they lived the good life, the *real life*—the life of the far north—the life of the 48th parallel. And it *was good.* Nobody to bother them, nobody to get in their way, nobody to tell them what to do. They just drank beer and ran wild and did whatever the hell they damn well pleased.

"Hey, look!" said Chet.

Howard glanced forward, then sat up on the seat. His eyes focused ahead on a huge animal—a mammoth of a beast—rising out of the ditch and then stopping on the upslope of the right hand shoulder. The animal stood large and majestic, it's great rack of antlers silhouetted in the gloomy grey air. Even from the distance they were at—nearly three, four hundred yards yet—they could see the creature's breath steaming lazily out over the roadway in heavy billowing puffs.

Chet and Howard's eyes lit up. Their faces simultaneously brightened. They both leaned forward towards the windshield and—as if on cue—began in unison, "Mum - mum - mum - mum - *moo-oo-oo-oo-oo-oo-oo-oose!*"—their lips protruding forward in sing-songy chant, followed by an outbreak of laughter—a punchy, adolescent, semi-drunken laughter...

Then the big creature started to move again. It lumbered forward to the top of the shoulder and then out onto the icy pavement—and the laughter immediately stopped. Chet and Howard's faces fell blank.

"Shit."

Chet quickly stepped down on the brakes, locking up all fours, which sent the pickup into a long slide, turning it into a bobsled on four rubber runners—gliding it down the glazed county highway at a steady 41 miles per hour—

The moose stopped broadside in the middle of the icy roadway, standing idly—and in the next moment Chet and Howard's faces drained *white*. Chet clutched the wheel tight, straight-arming himself up against the seatback—Howard planted his right hand on the dash, bracing his left elbow and hand against the backrest behind him—

"Son of a bitch."

"Shit."

Chet jammed his hand against the horn, sounding a weak insignificant little *humm* into the thick grey murk, which went ignored by the great beast. Howard stamped both his Sorel boots to the floor on the passenger side as if stamping down on the invisible brakes of a stage coach, standing himself right up against the seatback like Chet—

"Stop *this sonofabitch!*"

"I can't!"

Chet began frantically whipping the wheel back and forth, trying to steer out, pumping the brakes in panic—putting the pickup into a slight kilter—as the huge creature grew rapidly closer, approaching at a steady forty miles per hour, becoming a rising wall of colossal dark grey, it's majestic rack ascending higher and higher—

"Shit-shit-shit-"

Howard saw a wrinkle in the beast's sheeny blackish fur—then the slow blink of its eyeball—a scar on its upper leg—daylight under its mighty girth—his hand went to the door handle, then back to the dash—

"Shit!!! "

Then *CRASH!!!*—a massive *smashing* and *shattering,* and an abrupt jolt that *slammed* both Chet and Howard into the dash and windshield followed by the mammoth beast dropping onto the vehicle in a heavy grounding *crunch*. The impact of the massive animal *exploded* the windshield into a blast of glass shrapnel and pounded down on the front of the pickup in a *pulverizing grind* as if *squashing* it into the earth. The animal's hind-quarter vaulted up, over, and swung into the passenger side of the cab led by the rear hooves and legs which *bashed* in the door and window just as Howard dropped to the floor, followed by a second exploding shower of *shattering glass*. The head and rack of the beast whiplashed across and *crashed* into the driver's side of the cab—the left antler *smashing* through the driver's window, clipping Chet's Scottish cap right off the top of his head in the same instant he ducked to the floor—*smashing* out the remaining windshield from the inside out. The hind-quarter rebounded back over the hood and out over the road while the antlers remained lodged through the driver's door and windshield. The momentum of weight swung the pickup around in a dragging, spurning tackle, wrangling it around and around like a steer wrestler trying to pull it to the ground. The entire configuration of machine and beast slid down the road in a wobbling off-center spin, *twisting, pulling* and *groaning,* until a loud uprooting *crack* sounded, followed by the dismemberment and departure of Chet's entire side of the cab—door, frame, brackets, everything—all departing in a single *snap*—taking with it the beast's massive head and antlers and releasing from the vehicle a great substantial weight—which left Chet and Howard sliding light and free in a sudden onrush of cold air, as if someone had ripped the bedcovers off in winter time...

The tires of the rig finally caught some frozen shoulder gravel and the vehicle slowly skidded to a stop.

Chet and Howard remained hunched to the floor with transmission and engine parts rammed through the firewall between them. Chet reached up from the wreckage, felt around for the ignition, then switched it off—which killed the blowing of the heater fan and a faint clicking noise—leaving just a light *hissing* and *steaming*.

Howard brushed away broken glass and plastic, then lifted his head. He felt his face and neck for blood, then glanced around at the rest of the pickup. The cab was thoroughly mangled, crunched and heaved, reduced to a shell of crinkled metal, broken plastic and shattered glass...

"Jesus," he finally said, "that was one hell of a moose."

Howard looked over at Chet — who was in a ball beneath the buckled dash and twisted steering column. He started slowly pulling himself up.

"Hey Chet, you're bleedin'. On your head."

Chet touched his hand to his head, looked at the blood, then discounted it. His Scottish cap was gone, his blond bangs down in his eyes. Behind him, where his door had been, was now a collapsed porthole with flocked pine trees in the background. Everything seemed to stop. Time stopped. It was as if they had been suddenly jolted into a different place, a different world. A faint breath of winter air passed through the cab, ruffling the top of Chet's hair, followed by the sound of a long, anguished *moan*...

Howard pulled himself *up* onto the seat and looked out through the smashed out windshield cavity, then glanced to both sides, then turned around and looked out through what was left of the rear window, peering out between the shotguns which still hung miraculously in place on their rack.

"Holy shit..." Howard pulled on his door handle, then leaned against his door and gave it a shove, but it was mangled shut. He pulled himself up the remainder of the

way onto the seat, then crawled across the broken glass past Chet, stepping out through the open porthole and onto the road.

Not far to the back of the vehicle lay the huge pile of animal. It lay crossways in the middle of the road like a beached whale. Pieces of blue Ford metal and chrome lay scattered in between and littered beyond—all the way down the highway—pieces of fender and quarter panel... a mirror, a step board, part of an antler and smeared feces and *glass* everywhere.

"Jee-zez-Cure-eist," said Howard. He started towards the animal taking short, careful steps along the icy pavement. "Hey Stoolberg, get your ass out here!"

Chet pulled himself up, then worked his way out of the wreckage. As he emerged from the shambles and stepped onto the roadway, he slipped—his wing-tip shoes whisking straight up into the air, dropping him onto his back on the icy pavement. He cursed and swore—slipped and sprawled—then grabbed onto the side of the pickup, onto a piece of twisted metal and pulled himself back to his feet.

"*Look* at this thing, Chet! Holy balls, look at the *size* of this son of a bitch!"

Chet looked at Howard, then started towards him as if unable to look at his vehicle. His Hawaiian shirt bloomed fluorescent in the heavy murk, like a bright flower in a fog. He moved awkwardly—half-consciously— holding one hand to his hip, shuffling in short slippery steps as if on a hockey rink.

The moose lay on its back in front of Howard, its legs broken and limp—all four of them. Two were flapped out to the sides, lying loosely on the road in the wrong directions, and one lay twisted over its belly. The fourth was bent back under, wedged beneath the weight of its body and the road. The animal's head was cocked to the side, resting on damaged antlers and on the door of the pickup — which was forged around it's rack like a crinkled headdress. On the very high tip of one of the antlers hung Chet's Scottish cap. It looked as if someone had walked by and hung it there, as if hanging it on a hat tree. The animal's body was pulsating up and down in rapid breaths, a heavy grey steam billowing from its muzzle. Blood had formed around the mouth, and its eyes were wet, protruding and blinking... looking at Howard...

Chet stopped alongside Howard, then turned and looked back at his pickup. Howard shuffled closer to the moose, making a wide cautious arc around it, then approached from above, near the antlers. He bent over carefully at the waist and plucked Chet's cap from the high part of the rack.

"Hey Chet."

Chet turned and Howard flung him his cap—flinging it like a Frisbee. Chet caught it and put it back on his head, bloody hair and all. Then he turned from the moose and sat down right where he was—in the middle of the road. He sat facing his pickup, staring at it, putting his elbows on his knees and his hands on the sides of his head.

"Whata'ya think?" said Howard.

"I think we totaled my pickup."

"What about the moose, I mean? Whata'ya think we should do with him?"

"Shit," said Chet, saying it mostly to himself. "Shit. Shit. Shit. *Shit!!!*"

Howard kept staring at the moose. The animal was looking at him, breathing in a squeaky *wheeze* that sounded like a far off cry, a human cry. "You got any shells?"

"What?" said Chet. "No."

"I thought you had some."

"I told you when we left, I didn't have any."

"Yeah, but *none?* Not even *any?*"

"No."

"How 'bout in your pockets?"

"I haven't got any, Dunvold! Jesus."

"Well, shit," said Howard. He turned and looked down the road towards the Junction, then back the other way towards town. Nothing but whiteness and nothingness. "How 'bout a knife?"

"No."

"You haven't even got a knife?"

Chet turned to Howard. "Can't you hear?"

"Well yeah, but you should at least have a knife."

"Well what about *you*—where's *your* knife? Where's *your* goddamn shells? *Where's your goddamn brain!?—*"

The moose suddenly jerked upward, bucking its full girth into the air—then thumped heavily back down onto the pavement, shaking the entire roadbed beneath Howard and Chet. The animal let out a loud *hollering wail* causing Howard to flinch back, then slip and fall onto the ice. Both Chet and Howard scrambled back out of the way as the huge beast thrashed and flopped, flapping its legs like broken wings, *clanging* and *banging* its headdress of door metal on the icy pavement—

Jesus Christ!" said Howard, his voice rising an octave, his heart pounding up into his throat. He scrambled back to his feet. *"Holy goddamn shit!"*

Chet was also back on his feet, shuffling several steps

backwards.

"What have you got?" said Howard. "You got anything sharp, like a screwdriver, or something to hit him with?"

Howard started back towards the pickup, not waiting for an answer, taking fast creeping baby steps, scanning the wreckage as he approached, searching for *something—anything*—something sturdy—something jagged. But the only thing in sight was cheap metal and broken plastic. He went to the side of the box and looked in back; but just Chet's hip boots were there, and two gunny sacks of decoys. Then he spotted it: a tire jack. An old-fashioned stand-up type from Chet's old Impala. "How 'bout a tire jack?" He reached over and unclamped the jack from a make-shift bracket Chet had attached to the inside of the box, then started back with it.

Everything had become like a dream to Howard, a nightmare. He felt numb. He saw Chet standing near the moose, staring at it, his fluorescent yellow, orange, and purple glowing in the murk, the moose huffing and *wheezing* like a volcano building up pressure, preparing to blow again, its eyes reddish and strained—

"Here!" said Howard. He held the jack out to Chet. "You wanna do it?"

Chet looked at the jack, then at Howard. "Do *what?*"

"Kill him. I mean you're the one that hit the bastard."

"Well, I'm not going to stand out here in the middle of the road and clobber the goddamn thing with a tire jack."

"Well, what then? Whata'ya wanna do?"

"I don't give a shit," said Chet. "But if that's what *you want* to do, go ahead. I won't stop you."

"Well, it's not that I wanna clobber the thing either, but we gotta do something. I mean we can't just leave it like this. *Look at him."*

"Shit," said Chet. He had turned away and was looking back at his pickup again, arms folded. "Shit. Shit. Shit. *Shit!!!"*

Howard looked at the moose again and took a hesitant step towards it. "Well how do you think I should do it? I mean, where do you think I should hit him?"

"Where ever you want," said Chet. "Hit him on the head."

"The *head?* This little goddamn thing ain't gonna do shit to his head." The jack was one of the old ratchet type from the sixties—a three-and-a-half-foot piece of light tube-iron with a click-jack that climbed up and down, with a light square metal base at the bottom end. Howard began ratchet-lowering the jack part to the bottom of the stand, moving the weight—what little there was—to the one end.

Chet turned to Howard. "Then try the neck."

"The *neck?"* Howard said it like he had something sour in his mouth.

"Hit him with the corner piece of the stand," said Chet, "where it's sharp. Try to chop through to the jugular."

"Jesus Christ," muttered Howard, the sour thing still in his mouth. He shuffled closer to the beast, making that wide arc again—the moose's eyes following him, watching him move in from above, then stop alongside its antlers and the arrangement of crinkled blue door metal. Howard reached forward with the jack and poked at the animal, poking lightly, as if at a snake. The moose blinked and it's breathing grew quicker, *it's whining* louder, more distinct. Something seemed wrong to Howard. The creature's eyes didn't match its body anymore, they didn't seem like a moose's eyes—the way they were looking at him...

"What's that noise he's making?"

"Just hit the bastard," said Chet.

"It sounds like he's crying."

"Well he probably *is,*" said Chet—and he turned back to his pickup again.

Howard just stared at the moose, his own heart starting to pound again. The animal's *wheezing* was rising higher and sharper, coming from its open foaming muzzle—its eyes staring up at him, *begging him, pleading* with him...

"I don't like this."

"Oh, Jesus Christ!" said Chet. *"Just whack the goddamn thing!!!"*

Howard suddenly lifted the jack stand partway up like an ax. He held it at the high point of the motion for a moment—avoiding eye contact—then brought it down against the moose's neck, landing it in a dense *thunk*—which rebounded upward slightly as if Howard had swung it against a rubber padded wall.

The animal blinked, but didn't move.

"Harder!" said Chet.

"Shit," said Howard. He swallowed and rubbed at his nose, then raised the jack back up and swung down again—

Thunk!

The animal blinked again and flinched, raising its whine to a higher pitch.

"C'mon, *hit him,!*" said Chet.

"I am!"

"Well hit him harder!"

Howard raised up again and swung down hard, like a lumberjack, throwing all his weight into it—his boots slipping in mid-swing, landing the jack stand wide, sinking the corner bit into the jaw, tearing through hide and *chinking* into bone—and suddenly the beast *thrashed and bellowed* in a huge spasmic buck. Its head reared up and around catching Howard's leg with door metal, thrusting him to the ground, sending the tire jack flying from his hands. Howard landed on his back and immediately, instinctively, crouched his legs up into a tuck and began kicking wildly against the thrashing antlers and blue door metal—kicking in a mad panic, trying to push himself clear. He scrambled over onto his stomach and scurried away on all fours like a fallen bull rider. *"Holy-goddamn-shit,"* he said, crawling along the shoulder of the road, his heart pounding the air out of him. He finally collapsed to his side along the edge of the snowy pavement. Then he heard Chet—

"Goddamn bunch've shit—"

Howard turned to see Chet with the jack stand in hand, shuffling in his *wing-tips* straight towards the moose, moving directly up against the massive pumping body. Chet raised the jack high into the air then swung down hard in a solid *thud,* burying the metal corner into the beast's thick neck, producing a loud *agonizing moan* from the animal. He reached down and quickly retracted the piece, then raised up and swung down again—swinging furiously—producing another solid *thuck,* and a loud *shrilling wail.*

Howard pulled himself up onto all fours and started crawling back towards Chet and the moose. "Hey, Chet—"

Thuck—and another *wail bellowed* from the animal. Chet heaved up on the jack and then swung down again—swinging rapidly and wildly, chopping like an obsessed killer—a deranged madman in a Hawaiian shirt and Scottish cap—*thuck—thuck.*

"Hey, Chet, wait a second—"

The corner piece began ripping into throat tissue and blood began to splatter onto the jack.

"Wait—"

Thuck. Then the base of the jack stand flew off. It bounced down the icy road, going into a long slide like a curling rock. But Chet didn't miss a beat. He unchoked his grip and slid both hands to the one end, then raised up and swung down as if with a big stick or a baseball bat—*whack— whack— whack—*

"Wait a minute, Chet!"

Whack—whack—

"Stop!"

Chet stopped; but only because the beating was pointless. He quick-twirled the jack stand around like a baton and reversed his grip, sliding the heavy end down to his fists, clutching it like a long dagger; then he raised it up high over his head like a warring Centurion and drove downward into the beast's thick neck puncturing inward— drawing another *blood-curdling wail.*

"Aahh!" cried Howard. He turned away from it and closed his eyes. He could hear Chet behind him heaving up on the jack shaft, struggling to withdraw it from *suction.* When he opened his eyes again, he was looking downward at the November issue of *Sleaze Babe magazine—* at the *Babe of the Month* flung open over the roadway, her pale nude body sprawled over the centerline, lying amongst the diamonds of broken glass, her eyes still gazing up at *his—begging for it—*

Howard turned to Chet—just as Chet raised up and thrusted downward again, with everything he had, driving the jack shaft deep into the beast's thick neck. The puncture unleashed a wild buck and *scream* out of the animal and a simultaneous *hiss,* as if a high-pressure hydraulic hose had been punctured, followed by a spouting spray of fine red liquid and mist.

Chet shuffled backwards then slipped and fell to the pavement, scrambling back towards Howard on all fours—the warm spray of red speckling his face and cap and hair, speckling his Hawaiian shirt and Howard's coat, and speckling out over the *Babe of the Month's* pale nude body. Both Chet and Howard scurried further back on hands and knees, then turned to watch the beast's final moments—watching it *twist* and *thrash—gargling* and *choking*, its eyes protruding further and wider, *clanging* door metal against the pavement, its neck cinching and *wheezing* desperately for air.

Then the animal let out a final *scream—a chilling scream—*which amplified through both mouth and throat in dueling voices, spouting another fine red spray in twin spurting geysers. As the scream died, the beast began to settle, surrendering its last breath in a long *whimpering cry,* deflating itself of any remaining air. Its head shifted slightly, giving a final twist to the blue door metal of the Ford Motor Company... Then it slipped into silence, eyes open, locking its gaze upon the two with the thirst for the kill—the two that just drank beer and ran wild and did whatever the hell they damn well pleased...

***

That final scream was later said to have been heard all the way back to town. A woman crossing Main Street from the Piggly Wiggly store to the pharmacy with her two children later claimed that the scream had stopped the three of them in their tracks, right in the middle of the street. The woman said that the sound of the scream was eerie—unlike anything she'd ever heard—that it seemed to echo from far off, as if coming down from the heavens, and that it seemed to *hold* in the thick grey air...

***

A year later, during the following November, the geese were once again flocking by the thousands into Inquist's slough—once again congregating in the bogs and marshes in their great migration south. First, during the early part of the season, came the vast waves of Canadians and Blues, their flights scattered all across the sky from horizon to horizon; then later, during the following month, came the great waves of fluttering *white*—the vast expansive flights of Swans and Snows...

But for many miles along Inquist's slough there were only the sounds of sanctuary, only the sounds of blowing winds, of fluttering wings, and of the birds' thousands of lonely voices honking and calling out to one another...

There was no gunfire waiting for them...

Howard Dunvold hadn't been out.

And Chet Stoolberg still hadn't fired his new gun.

A TRIP BACK DOWN

Winter 1986

The end of Lewy Olson's career arrived on a Sunday morning.

It came during his eleventh season, shortly after he paid an unwelcomed visit to a local sportswriter's house—which resulted in criminal charges filed against him for breaking and entering, and for attempted murder. Although the charges were later reduced to assault and battery, the ruling from the NHL was permanent expulsion, which forever banished Olson from the League. At thirty-two, he was out of a job. He had nowhere to go, so he set out on a three week drunk, spent mostly in the downtown district, which was interrupted only by a couple court appearances and the morning meetings with his attorney. At the end of the third week Olson listed his townhouse in Highland Park with *Steel City Reality*, then packed up eleven years' worth of belongings and headed home for the remotes of northern Minnesota where he went to work in the stick factory and began a new effort of trying to adjust.

Unlike Pittsburgh, Olson's hometown was small. It was a border town, without stoplights or convenience stores. It had no fast foods or any buildings over two stories. Along the westerly edge of the community stood the only actually *new* building in the area, which was a modern one-level structure made of white and blue poly-buffed steel. Displayed across the front of the building were the five multi-colored Olympic hoops and big red letters which proudly said:

HARTJI BROS. HOCKEY STICKS
LUEFTEN, MN
HOCKEYTOWN, USA

Olson was assigned to an inspection station near the center of the plant. It was a mid-level position—given to him because of *who he was*, and because of the several years he'd worked in the old plant as a kid. The plant had now become a large myriad of clinically clean machines, presses and conveyors that throbbed, banged and pulsated, producing sticks quickly—processing bare cut lumber into a color-schemed, eye-catching product, with HARTJI USA printed across the stick shafts—HARTJI in bold red print, and USA in blue.

Following his shift each day, Olson walked the snow-banked streets of Lueften—walked past the lumberyard and the café—then stopped for drinks at Bernie Fisherman's Bar. Fisherman's was an old, hole-in-the-wall tavern, located next door to the city arena. It was a small, dark, smoky little place, named after and owned by the famous half-breed

Indian who had played for the Chicago Blackhawks.

Inside Fisherman's, the clientele was not pretty. It was a rough looking bunch that ranged in age from early twenties to late forties. They loitered about in a murky haze—surrounded by bottles, cigarettes, and mixed drinks; their faces silent, scarred, and unshaven; their eyes bloodshot, empty, and lost. Some of the eyes occasionally sparked into animation—fueled by liquor and the retelling of old stories—while others yielded quietly to the inevitable state of defeat. These were the forgotten ones. Yesterday's heroes, society's castaways. All around them on the walls hung their jerseys—mostly red, white and blue USA jerseys, some professional. Large blow-up pictures hung like Grand Prix action photos—shots of high-speed body checks, great plays, victories, and moments of glory. Dozens of game sticks also lined the walls—*victory sticks*—magic-markered across the shafts with dates, cities, and scores that spanned decades and cities around the world—Stockholm - Sapporo - Vienna - Lake Placid - Moscow - Helsinki - Bucharest...

Upon Olson's arrival, he had initially been popular at Fisherman's. His Pittsburgh jersey was pinned prominently to the wall and the celebration was extensive. But after a few days the novelty wore off, and then gradually, without warning or fanfare, he slowly became a regular.

Olson began spending his afternoons at the bar, mostly talking to Bernie himself—who usually leaned onto his elbows from the other side, a patch over one eye, his long black hair resting onto his shoulders. Fisherman's career had ended several years back, after a high stick on the ice in St. Louis, which resulted in the loss of that left eye. Above Bernie, over the mirrors and bottles, hung a large poster-size picture of him in his legendary NHL uniform—*The Great Bernie Fisherman,* in the famous red, black and gold of the Chicago Blackhawks— clean-cut, young, and dazzling.

Bernie talked mostly about making a *come-back,* or of maybe joining the local semi pro team, the Lueften Lakers. As the afternoons wore on, he often became drunker and louder—and then began to repeat himself—after which, Olson usually left.

From Fisherman's, Olson often headed towards the park, strolling out onto the narrow peninsula that projected itself out onto the bay of Lake of the Woods. He meandered through the stark white snow and dormant grey elms— wandering methodically and routinely—usually towards the outdoor rink, and as he did, he thought about who he had been for the last thirty-two years, thought about who he had been for the last eleven years, thought about who he had been only a few months back.

A sportswriter had once described him as a cross between Leif Ericson and a Hells Angel. But he had been more commonly known—in and around the NHL—as simply a *fighter, as a goon*—as the bad man from Pitt. He had been known as the *Big Nordic Outlaw*—the one who had led the League in fights, fines, and penalties—the one who had garnered enough lawsuits against himself and against the Pittsburgh Penguins to demand that the team not only re-fortify its insurance policies, but triple its legal staff.

It had been said by some that Olson's career had been one of the most notorious in NHL history, that he had brought a level of violence to Pittsburgh—and into the League—that was unparalleled anywhere in the game.

But the fact was, he had brought *color* to Pittsburgh.

He had brought victory, entertainment and excitement. He had helped to bring a struggling young team out of the cellar and into Stanley Cup contention—not to mention a twenty percent increase in gate attendance, and a significant rise to the team's television ratings.

Olson stopped alongside the outdoor rink to watch a group of young boys playing on the ice. They wore big snow pants and stocking caps, and imitated moves that were above their level. The boys were maybe eleven or twelve, their voices young and eager, echoing through the park as they called out for passes.

Olson sized up the rink itself, which was the same now as it had always been—tired, old, and aging. The boards were grey-weathered planks, set vertically all the way around—then boarded over the top and along the back with heavy support lumber. The planks were warped and blistered with wide gaps and rotted knots, filled in with tight-packed snow that was banked-up from behind.

Early in the season, when the snow was still light, the pucks made *sharp* echoes through the park when fired against the planks; but then, as the season lingered on and the snow piled deeper from endless shovelings, the sounds of the shots gradually lowered, eventually becoming dull thuds against the thick, dense weight behind.

As Olson eyed the rink, he recalled specific boards and knots from his childhood—*targets* he had spent endless hours shooting at, trying to hone his accuracy. Looking back on it now, it had been a long, hard, difficult road, from shooting pucks at those knots and dreaming of being a pro, to making it even as far as the high school team, the *Lueften Nordics*. It had been a long ways again from the Lueften Nordics to Team USA, and a long ways again from there to the majors. Yes, it had been a long, hard road from the cold, lonely silence of this little rink, to the *packed roaring crowds of Pittsburgh Civic* where he would throw a sudden hip check—decking an oncoming attacker—and draw a spontaneous, *thunderous roar* from 16,000 people, and the many thousands of others watching on television. Yes, it had been a long, hard, endless struggle to finally get to the top—to finally get to that place of childhood dreams...

... But the trip back down was also hard. And there were times like these, standing unnoticed in the snow, watching the young aspiring stars of tomorrow, that it felt even harder.

The morning shift at the stick factory was processing one of the last batches of the *Haasen Autogragh*—one of the last of that particular model that would ever be produced. The sticks passing Olson's eye were freshly cut—without fiberglass, print, or trim on yet—just the bare, rough stick, evenly spaced along a slow conveyor belt. As Olson scrutinized the sticks for warps and fractures, he thought about the player whom the stick had been named after: *the greatest player ever to put on a pair of skates,* Tommy Haasen.

Haasen had been the brilliant young sensation who was destined to shatter all the records and revolutionize the game. He was the young athletic genius who had possessed the magical, musical play, who had been titled by the media and hailed by the public as, *"The American Magician."* He was the mega-superstar—the one who had caught the eyes and captured the hearts of people all around the world—the one who, in almost the next moment, was *gone.*

Disappeared. Finished.

Haasen had gotten off the road early, while there was still

plenty of it in front of him. He had made his exit nearly three years back, on a snowy night in Minneapolis—did it with a .38 caliber Smith & Wesson.

Olson had entertained similar thoughts himself, but so far he had lacked the courage—which struck him as rather pathetic, because courage was not something he was supposed to be short of.

Tommy Haasen, on the other hand, had just not seemed the type. Like Olson, he had been a hometown boy—had started in the toddler league—had played Peewees, had been a star on the high school team, the *Lueften Nordics.*

But unlike Olson, Haasen had been *perfect.* He had been special—a *one and only.* He was a small, twinkly-eyed kid—a pleasant kind of kid who had gone through life surrounded by a *glow, a light.* He had become a starter for Team USA—and it was around that time that the phenomena hit and the media attention boomed—that the magazine covers started, and the million dollar offers began. Then the signing with Detroit...

Olson glanced behind him to the bare cut lumber funneling into the prep area, then ahead of him towards the bundles of finished product, all stacked and bound and ready for crating. The Haasen Autograph was by far the flashiest stick Hartji's had ever put out. The model was detailed in red, white, and blue—the top third in dark blue with white clustered stars, and the lower section in red with white elongated letters running down, reading USA but artistically distorted, emanating the effect of red and white stripes wavering in the wind. It was the first and only autographed stick Hartji's had ever produced—and it was *that signature* signed along the shaft of stars and stripes, in thin black cursive, that had caused the craze. In its prime, the stick had sold in unprecedented numbers—selling all across Canada, the northern United States, and Europe, selling in masses—not so much to upper level players in the high school, college, or professional ranks, but rather to anxious young boys whose eyes were seduced by the flashy colors, and who aspired to one day be as great—or at least be temporarily in their minds as great—as their idol who used the stick—the greatest player ever to live: *The American Magician.*

Olson contemplated the colorful bundled squares of Haasen Autographs across the plant, looking like rows of coffins with wrinkled American flags draped over, ready and waiting to be shipped.

The big sales boom had come to a close. The awestruck eyes of young boys had dimmed and were now gazing up at other heroes. The attraction was gone; the markets were lost. And the stick that had been autographed by the greatest player of all time, the stick that had been the largest selling hockey stick in the entire world, had now hit the end of its line...

Which would now be discontinued...

And eventually, forgotten.

Olson got drunk at Fisherman's again. He drank a toast to Tommy Haasen, and said goodbye to his stick, the *Haasen Autograph.*

By the time he left the bar, darkness had fallen, so he wandered the snow-banked walks of Lueften under the blue-tinted glow of humming streetlights. He eventually ended up at the park again—where again he stood alone in the snow alongside the old rink.

The rink lay vacant in a white-dusted gloss. The goals

sat slightly askew, rusted, and bent—just recently abandoned. It was getting late. Saturday night. The last had left until morning.

Olson watched his breath rise slowly in the rink light. He heard voices... *Teenage voices*. He glanced towards the warming house, which sat off to one end of the rink, down a short, snow-shoveled path. It was a one room shack with lazy smoke drifting from a kiltered stack. Still the same.

The lights over the rink were the same too—an old array of green chinaman hat lamps that arced out over the ice on skinny rusted poles.

Olson focused on the pole nearest the warming house, on the switch rigged to the side. The first person in the morning used to switch them on, and the last to leave at night would flip them out.

Years ago—before the Pittsburgh Penguins, before Team USA, and before the Lueften Nordics—a small boy would switch those lights on each morning—and often times, he would be the one to flip them out again at night. The boy would walk down to the rink every morning in the early darkness, open the warming house and build a fire in the stove, then put on his skates, turn on the lights and start to skate. He was always at the rink long before the other boys; the others usually skated for an hour before school and then a couple at night, but *he* always skated *two* before school and *several* at night. He skated twice as long as the other boys and twice as hard, because his heart was set on being the best—the *very best*—on being the greatest of them all.

Many mornings the boy had to shovel snow in order to clear enough space to stickhandle and shoot, and sometimes it was so cold that he was the only one there. The others usually came until the temperatures dropped to fifteen or twenty below zero, but after that they wouldn't show.

But the little boy whose heart was set on greatness was there. He was *always there.* Thirty-eight below zero and he was there—building a fire in the stove and lacing up his skates—bundled in snow pants, stocking cap, and mittens, then skating under the lights—all alone— surrounded by the cold silent darkness. He'd skate up and down the glossy little rink at a hard, relentless pace, stickhandling the puck out in front of himself, prancing side to side in crossover steps, deking and maneuvering, firing the puck at targeted knots in the boards, then picking it up as it careened off and around, throwing some head and shoulder dekes, just like the big guys, then cutting back around again, working feverishly hard—up and down, up and down, non-stop— until he was grunting and sniffling and his little legs were lagging like lead and his head was drooping and the sub-zero frost was biting at his feet and the pain was telling him to quit. But then somewhere inside of him, somewhere deep down within, he would find the spirit and the strength to struggle on—a whole packed arena surrounding him, *cheering him on*—his steamy breath pumping out of him, freezing in a white frost along the wool of his hat, coughing and whimpering from exhaustion, but struggling on... *struggling on...*

Often, on those cold mornings, the boy ended up on the floor of the warming house holding his frozen stocking feet near the warmth of the stove, nursing them with his small hands. He'd bite down hard against the thawing pain, his eyes clenched tightly against seeping tears—his skates, boots, and mittens lying about him on the floor.

Afterwards, he'd sling his skates and stick up over his shoulder, then follow the shoveled path to the end light pole, where his mitten would reach up to flip out the switch, leaving the dull, hazy light of morning all around him. Sometimes he'd remain there for an extra moment to look through the park trees, across the big frozen lake—to the cold orange glow dawning in the east... It was the beginning of another day; and he was one step closer to becoming one of the *greats*. And the next day would be the same, and he would be yet another step closer. And the day after that would be the same again, and he would be yet another step closer. And he would continue to work and dream and struggle and follow the path, stepping closer and closer, until one day... he would be *there*.

The great players of the game—the *stars*—were the most cherished, most loved people in the world. Nobody received more adoration than the great ones—and the thought of all that love gave the boy strength. It gave him endless strength.

Yes, he too would become one of the greats, and one day, he too would have all that love.

The boy was determined.

His heart was set.

His name was Lewy Olson. And he was going to be the greatest of them all.

Olson heard the *voices* again. He glanced again at the warming shack where a single light bulb glowed from the lone framed window, and smoke drifted upward from the kiltered stack...

Olson opened the door of the warming house and stepped inside, and as he did, a teenage boy sitting on a bench quick-stuffed his hand behind his back.

"Hey, Lewy," said the boy, and he flashed a quick

smile. There were three of them—two boys and a girl. All three looked at Olson, eyes alert. Olson stood in the doorway, sensing the air, the smoke.

"What the hell you guys doin' in here?"

"Huh?" said the boy.

"Nothin'," said the second boy. "It's the stove, it leaks."

Olson didn't look at the stove, he just looked at the three teenage kids. They all sat on the same bench, their backs against the wall. The two boys wore skates and big Air Force flight pants with high suspenders strapped over their parkas. Their hair was wedged and sweaty, their sticks lying against the bench alongside them. One of the boys wore a fur fox hat, propped high on his flushed head, his arm around the girl who sat in between them. The girl wore a red, white, and blue Lueften Nordics letter jacket, with crossed hockey sticks on the upper sleeve.

Olson closed the door behind him and walked in across the scuffed wooden floor. He sat down on the adjacent bench.

"You guys aren't doin' so good this year."

The boys didn't respond. Then one of them said, "No," in a downcast tone.

"We ain't got no seniors," said the other boy.

That's no excuse, Olson wanted to say, but then didn't.

The boy without the hat then shifted himself on the bench and cleared his throat. "Hey, did ya hear that Nute got a letter from the pros?"

Olson looked at Nute, the boy with the fox hat.

"New York Rangers!" said the first boy proudly. "Tell 'em, Nute."

"It's nothin'," said Nute. He shrugged shyly and adjusted his fox hat, and the girl under his arm smiled proudly.

"He's invited to their training camp!" said the first boy. "Soon as he graduates."

Olson nodded to himself, then looked down at the flickering glow at the base of the stove. It was quiet. Just a light crackling of the fire...

Then Nute took his arm out from behind the girl and leaned forward onto his knees. He looked at Olson, about to speak, but then looked downward and searched the floor. He readjusted his fox hat once more, then looked at Olson again.... Then he said: "What's it like in the big leagues, Lewy? I mean, the pros?" He cleared his throat and swallowed, then continued carefully. "I mean, um... you think I can make it?"

Olson looked at the boy... then looked back at the stove again. "I don't know," he said.

The stove was still the same. So was the pile of wood in the corner. The same boarded floor, scuffed to a fuzz from the countless years of endless skate traffic. The same light bulb at the center of the ceiling with the same string hanging down. The same smell of burning birch and wet snow. It was all the same. All except *him*. He'd come out the other side.

"I used to skate down here every night just like you guys," Olson said, "ever since I was a little kid. Every night I'd come down here, and every morning too, before school, and I'd turn on the lights and I'd start skating and I'd dream about the *big leagues*. I'd dream of being a *pro*... That's all I ever thought about. It's all I ever wanted."

Olson stared for a moment into the amber glow flickering along the floor. Then he said... "But I just didn't have it."

Olson took a big breath and released it... Then he continued, "I had to fight and play cheap to make it. I never really *had it*... I never had it like you've got it, Nute. You're gifted. I've seen you skate. I've seen you move the puck... but I don't know."

Olson ran his big hands up over his face and then looked at the boy again. Then he said, "All I know is this: that there's at least a hundred other guys out there right now that got *invites* just like you. And they're just as fast as you and just as quick—they're just as good, and they're hungry, and they want it as bad as you, and some even worse. And when you leave here you're gonna meet those guys, and when you *do,* you're gonna find that the line between the ones who make it and the ones that don't, is very, very thin. *And if you don't make it*... then all the time you spent down here, all the mornings, all the nights, all the twenty below zero, all the practices and games in the arena, all the pucks you've shot over the summers, all the sweat and pain you've given the game won't matter anymore, 'cause it'll all be over. And then you can come back here and you can sit in this little place and you can smoke that shit you're smokin' all you want. You can smoke it and smoke it 'til you can't tell up from down. 'Cause nothing will matter anymore. And nobody will care."

Nute swallowed a lump in his throat.

All three teenagers sat motionless, eyes to the floor...

Olson got up and ambled back towards the door. He stopped and took another breath... then looked back again before going out...

"And that's what it's like, Nute."

THE GIFT

Letegorsk, Russia
Union of Soviet Socialist Republics
December 1972

Every day, the mothers of the nine-and-ten-year-olds gathered along the boards at the old community arena to gossip and socialize while their sons played on the ice in front of them. The same women had been meeting along the boards for several years—congregating in their heavy coats, hats, and mufflers—ever since their boys had started in the toddler league together. Living in a northern hockey town as small and remote as Letegorsk lended the women to knowing each other intimately well, and so much of their lives—as well as the lives of others—were commonly planned, discussed, and reviewed while gathered at the rink during their boys' daily ice times.

One day, a *new* woman appeared at the arena. She came with her son, a *new boy,* helped him lace and tighten his skates, and then joined the other women along the boards as her child happily took to the ice with the others.

But the Letegorsk women did not acknowledge this new, intruding woman. They ignored her, pretending not to notice, and did not include her in their conversations.

The word around town was that this new woman's name was Mrs. Kershy, and that she had just moved from the city of Leningrad—*alone*—with her child, this *new* little boy. Mrs. Kershy was a very young looking woman, trim and petite, with a soft, shy face—which the Letegorsk women found deliberately postured and *deceitful.* To them, it was quite obvious who she was; she was one of those ungrateful few who had been obnoxiously blessed with all the perfect features of a Nordic midnight sun girl. Her arrogant beauty offended the Letegorsk women, as did her manner of dress— *Western fashions,* obviously purchased from exclusive peddlers in Leningrad—*Who did she think she was!* It was also no secret that all the men in Letegorsk were certainly *staring* at her and *gawking* over her and that the men at the sawmill were making lewd comments about her—and the thought of some of these comments was utterly *repulsive* to the Letegorsk women. The women had no place amongst them for a scandalous city girl such as this, and so they continued not to notice her, and in their own subtle ways were even impudently rude to her.

By the third practice, the new woman from Leningrad—having been ousted by the others—stood alone, down near the corner of the rink, behind the old wire-mesh backstop.

But she continued to come. Each day, she would bring her little boy to the arena, help him lace and tighten his skates, then take his hand and walk with him from the warmth of the lobby into the frigid freshness of the arena, down the wooden stairs, and then take her place in the corner to watch him play with the other boys, while the group of townswomen all stood along the boards between the red and blue lines gossiping and whispering about her. She was a *typical, uppity city girl,* the women had all decided; and she was *obviously snobbish* and felt she was better than them. They gossiped about her little boy too— the one she brought to the rink. There was clearly something *wrong* with the child, obviously a problem since birth, they had all determined. He was terribly small and frail—only *half the size* of the other boys in the league—obviously stunted of growth. He also had several other deficiencies, *learning deficiencies*—he couldn't even tighten his own skates yet, his *beautiful mother* still had to help him! The little boy was certainly a good player, the townswomen all agreed—an exceptional player—but he would not be able to continue much longer, as he would not grow and develop like the other boys in the league and would soon have to drop out.

And so it continued, every day, for several weeks—the townswomen along the boards gossiping and gabbing about the uppity city girl with the freakish little boy. *It was fitting,* some of them had decided; *it was justice in the universe* that a woman who thought that she was *so beautiful* and *so glamorous* and *so much better than everyone else,* ended up with a freak child.

But then came a day when the scuttle and gossip along the boards in Letegorsk all came to an abrupt halt. It happened when news hit town that this new little boy from Leningrad was not stunted of growth at all. The word that ascended upon the remote little village and then buzzed through the snow-filled streets, said that the little boy—Yuri Kershy—had been a *major* sensation in Leningrad, and that officials there had directed Mrs. Kershy to move to the northern hockey town of Letegorsk, and that they had instructed the coaches in Letegorsk to put Yuri in with the nine-and-ten-year-olds. The townswomen learned that the Kershy boy, who they thought was deficient and stunted of growth, was not deficient of anything, but was only very young—he was not yet a nine-or-ten-year-old like *their* boys. The women learned that the Kershy boy was in fact, *considerably* younger—that he was not yet an eight-year-old, or even a seven-year-old. The word was, that this new little boy with the beautiful mother—who the townswomen had never once spoken to, who they had chosen to ignore and be deliberately rude to—was only *six years old,* and that according to the coaches in Leningrad, was the most spectacular player for his age that they had ever seen.

The Letegorsk women quickly adjusted their attitudes. They immediately began introducing themselves to Mrs. Kershy, and welcomed her in amongst them, and when they *did...* they found that she was not at all what they had determined her to be. They found that she was not uppity or snobbish at all, but that her soft, shy face was in fact sincere. She was a very quiet, very kind young woman, and when the townswomen spoke to her, she smiled warmly at them and her green eyes seemed to twinkle. And when they complimented her on her son, Yuri—which was frequently—she often blushed and looked downward, in an almost adolescent, school-girlish sort of way.

But as spectacular as Mrs. Kershy's little boy was, he seemed to improve and mature even further by the day, developing more sophistication in his skating and stickhandling—becoming smoother, quicker, faster. There were many excellent players in the hockey town of Letegorsk, but none that had the natural grace, speed, and the incredibly rare instincts that little Yuri Kershy had. By age eight, he was playing with the same boys in the eleven-and-twelve-year-old league, and at this age was capable of controlling, not only complete offensive rushes, but entire games. Yuri's true strength however was still as a team player. He networked fully with his mates, often tallying more assists than goals, which made him popular, not only amongst the other boys in Letegorsk, but amongst the general citizenry as well. Also by age eight, Yuri's unique movements of skates and stick had begun to stupefy the townspeople, displaying before their very eyes, miraculous moves which they had never before witnessed, moves they found difficult to understand or even comprehend. It was almost as if the little boy was... *magical.*

Soon, word began to spread to other northern villages of this spectacular little boy with the special movements. The stories traveled far and wide, eventually seeping southward into the larger towns, and then into the cities, and eventually into Moscow. Soon, scouts began to arrive in Letegorsk, first coming from the lower league teams, and then later from the major league teams—all coming to see for themselves if these exaggerated claims they had been hearing held any truth or merit.

By mid-winter of that year, the little village of Letegorsk had filled with a spirit of pride and flattery that it had never before experienced. The townspeople basked in a reveling glow of prominence and honor as some of the nation's most prestigious scouting officials graced their village—all coming to *their* little town, to see one of *their* boys—*and a boy of only age eight!*

And come they did that year, arriving in ones and twos, and sometimes even threes—representing most all the major teams from the Soviet National Elite League. Scouts came from the Dynamo teams and from the Soviet Wings; they came from the Gorki Torpedos, and from the Spartak team, and from Traktor; and from one of Yuri's favorites, the Krystal team.

But none of the excitement and celebration that year matched the fervor and exhilaration that swept the little village one day late in the season, almost spring, when word traveled up and down through the slush-filled streets that scouts had arrived in Letegorsk representing the most prestigious, most elite team in the land: The Central Red Army of the Soviet Union.

The little town lit in a glowing stir matched by nothing of the preceding months. The townspeople milled in the streets and markets, muddling with gossip and speculation, then flocked to the arena that afternoon, nearly packing it, just to see the prominent Red Army scouts watch their special little boy. As play began, the arena fell still, nearly silent, leaving only low whispering voices, the sounds of skates and sticks, and hundreds of eyes shifting between little Yuri Kershy and the two scouts. The scouts were dapper looking men, stolid in long winter trench coats. They stood in the players boxes studying the boy with expressionless faces, occasionally exchanging words and jotting notes—and then after the session, spoke with him in the lobby of the arena, where once again the townspeople huddled around to listen and gawk. The scouts asked questions of little Yuri, who stood holding his mother's hand, gazing upward with twinkling green eyes and responding in the sweet voice of a young bird. As Yuri spoke, he pointed to his gathered teammates, telling the scouts that they were all very good players, and probably the reasons his scoring averages were so high. Each time one of the elite scouts glanced at a boy being pointed out, the mother of the child would flush with a flattery and a pride that would probably be remembered for the rest of her life. It was a thrill for Yuri too, to speak to these men. Yuri's two heroes, whose posters hung over his bed, both played for the Central Red Army; they were, Gvesik Trotsky and Valeri Kharlamov. Yuri asked the men if they got to see Trotsky and Kharlamov play in person, at the Sports Palace; and to this, the men and the townspeople laughed, and then the men told Yuri that yes, they did get to see them in person, and quite often.

By age thirteen, Yuri Kershy was playing with the upper boys' team in Letegorsk, and it was during that year that he was chosen to play for the Soviet Youth All Stars. The All Stars were selected from all across the country and then assembled in Moscow where they lived in dormitories and studied hockey together—as well as academics—for a period of two months. Each of the boys chosen was exceptionally gifted, all showing promise of one day playing in the Soviet National Elite League. As All Stars, the boys studied, practiced, and drilled daily on all aspects of hockey. They studied with the masters and experts of the game and were coached by some of the country's finest. The boys viewed game films, read books, studied graphs, geometrical charts, and statistics. They trained rigorously—on and off the ice—and in the gym, and played a strenuous schedule of engagements with a variety of other teams, including higher level teams in the Soviet Union as well as Youth All Star teams from other countries, such as Czechoslovakia, Finland, and Romania. The boys studied the game from an International perspective, studying different players, teams, and countries, scrutinizing various styles of play—theories and philosophies—breaking everything down into the game's most miniscule details, into its beats and measures and rhythms, dissecting and examining it from multiple angles and points of view—and then reassembling it, putting it all back together again, searching to understand its most integral movements, its *heart,* and its *flow.*

It was during this time, while in Moscow studying with the Youth All Stars, that Yuri Kershy learned of a player that abruptly caught his attention. Yuri had heard of the player before—he had seen his picture and knew of his rising greatness—but his complete and undivided attention was suddenly captured by the new star while in the classroom one morning studying game films with the other boys. The particular film the boys were viewing was of the current USA team playing the Canadians, and what Yuri saw on the screen that morning changed his life. The player was the one the boys had all been talking about and stirring over. He was an American—the one who wore the number *seven*—the new sensation of the game that was being touted as not only the greatest player in the world, but as the greatest player ever to put on a pair of skates. He was the one they were calling: *The American Magician.*

Yuri's eyes settled into the screen in a twinkling green, hypnotic stare, following the mystical movements back and forth, witnessing a brilliance in beautiful flowing red, white, and blue that he had never before seen or felt. He was enraptured. Completely. The player moved with a swiftness and grace that seemed to originate out of some form of divine instinct, or power. It was like magic—except not just *talk magic—real magic.* The player possessed instincts and sensibilities that were from someplace beyond—far more developed than anything Yuri had ever known or heard of—far above even Gvesik Trotsky's, or Sergei Mikilov's, or even the great Valeri Kharlamov's.

After that day, Yuri could not stop thinking about what he had seen. He thought about the American player constantly, in a continuous, almost dreamy, preoccupied state. He lay in bed, nights, re-running in his mind over and over the miraculous swiftness, style, and grace that he had seen on the screen—seen with his very own eyes. The player moved as if everything around him was in slow motion. It was like he sensed the other movements before they were happening, as if he were encased in a protective, haloed glow... He seemed to float... There was truly something special about the player, something extraordinary, something... *magical.*

Yuri asked his instructors if he could see the film again.

Then he asked to see other films of the Americans, and then begged to see more, asking to see them again and again. Yuri studied the films endlessly during the weeks that followed, becoming increasingly obsessed with what he saw. He began to memorize the movements—*The Magician's* shifts, his rhythms and flow—searching to feel in himself a similar *likeness*—if there indeed was such a likeness—searching to feel an understanding, a *connection.*

Yuri's growing obsession with *The American Magician* began to draw curiosity and questions from the other boys, and when Yuri tried explaining it to them, they seemed to not understand. They all certainly recognized The Magician's brilliance and greatness, but to Yuri, they saw only the *results* of that greatness; they failed to see the nucleus, the true genius that was creating the phenomenon.

Yuri became frustrated trying to explain his fascination to the others, and so he wrote to his mother and explained it to her. Yuri always told his mother about his hopes and dreams and about his worries and troubles, and she always listened and always seemed to understand. He told her in the letter that this player had become a new influence on his game, and that he had found in him a silent mentor—a mentor who was giving him a whole new inspiration and focus to his life—and that with this discovery of *The American Magician,* and with all the knowledge and experience he was gaining in Moscow, that the Youth All Stars had become a thrilling, yet pinnacle point of importance in his career.

But then heartbreak came to Yuri.

It came during the final weeks of the Youth All Star assembly when the team's big surprise was announced:

that they would be traveling West, beyond the Wall, to Stockholm, Sweden, to take part in an International Youth hockey tournament with several *Western* teams participating! There would be Youth All Star teams from Sweden, Norway, Denmark, Finland, Holland, Czechoslovakia, and even a team from Canada! The trip was announced only a week before the boys were to leave, and the news filled them with such excitement that they could hardly control themselves.

But then Yuri fell ill with the flu. His temperature shot into a high fever and he had to remain behind, in bed, as the others all departed for Scandinavia. Yuri's spirits were crushed, and his mother—sensing his despair over the telephone—soon arrived in Moscow on the overnight train, her suitcase in hand, to stay with Yuri in his dormitory until he was well.

During that week, Yuri's mother sat at his bedside and consoled his sadness, stroking his hair and telling him that there would be other opportunities to travel and to play with the boys from the other countries. Yuri listened closely to his mother as she spoke, his sweaty head lying on the pillow, his twinkling eyes beaming up through the fever. He had her eyes—the very same—except his seemed to have little crystals inside that made them always twinkle, no matter what he was feeling. His mother suddenly felt so proud of him; so very proud—not because of his athletic abilities or accomplishments, but because he was such a good child; such a warm, kind, and loving child. She felt her heart begin to swell and fill her with a deep rushing warmth, and then her eyes began to well. She looked away, wiping her hand across her face, and then suddenly leaned forward again, clutching Yuri upward into her arms, hugging him tightly, holding his sweaty young head against her neck with all of her strength.

She sat with Yuri all of that week, caring for him—speaking to him and listening to him—and it was during this time that Yuri told her in lengthy detail about *The American Magician*. He told her about the great player's movements and instincts—which he said he had been dreaming about even in his sleep, even with the fever. He told her that he was trying to feel the same instincts and reflexes in himself, and that he wanted to learn to play the same as The Magician did, and that as soon as he was better, that he even wanted to change his jersey number; that from now on, he wanted to be number *seven*—the same as *The Magician*.

The next week, the All Star boys returned to Moscow, and Yuri, having recovered from his illness, returned to practice. When he first saw his teammates in the locker room, they all ran to him and surrounded him in a stir of excitement, anxious to tell about their trip to Sweden. They had gone undefeated at the tournament, taking first place, followed by Sweden and Canada, and then Czechoslovakia. But it wasn't their trophy or victories that they were so anxious to tell about, it was something else; something bigger. They all began telling in excited overlapping voices about the big treat they had all been given while in Stockholm: the USA National team had been in the country at the very same time to play the Swedish Nationals, *and they all got to go to the game!*

At this, Yuri's heart sank. He thought he was going to cry, but his fascination with what the boys were telling him held him from tears.

"We all got tickets, and we had very good seats," said one of the boys, "down in the corner, close to the ice and so we saw him up close!"

"Very close!" said another boy.

"And if we wouldn't have been given the reserved tickets, we never would have been able to go because the game was sold out for weeks ahead and people outside were selling their tickets for big sums of money, and there were all these girls there, hundreds of them—"

"*Thousands* of them!" corrected another boy. "They were inside the arena and outside—all Swedish girls that came to see *him!* Only to see *him!*"

The boys were so full of excitement and talking so fast and over the top of one another that Yuri could hardly understand them. They had been overwhelmed with what they had seen, and next, began demonstrating for Yuri some of the moves The Magician had made, showing with their sticks on the locker room floor, and explaining with their hands, searching for the words to describe the incredibility of what had taken place.

"He controlled the game!" one explained. "They defeated the Swedes, four to one, and the Swedes were clearly the stronger team but they could not contain The Magician!"

"He scored three times!" shouted another boy.

And then they told Yuri how the next day they all got to go to the big luxury hotel in Stockholm called the *Globe,* where the Americans were staying, and how The Magician was in a big ballroom full of T.V. cameras and reporters, and all the Youth teams were there because they had all been promised a chance to get his autograph! The boys told Yuri how The Magician sat at a big table full of microphones, and of all the Swedish girls, hundreds of them—no, thousands of them—mobbed around him, and how they were all in love with him and how there were many, many policemen there just to keep the girls from rushing him. The boys all nodded long and hard to this so that Yuri would believe them, as incredible as it sounded. They told Yuri that if *they,* themselves, had not been given a special reserved time to see The Magician, that they never would've gotten close to him. They told of how he was in the ballroom for almost two hours answering questions of reporters and signing autographs at the same time and talking and smiling to all the kids and to all the boys from all the Youth teams from all the different countries. *He was very nice,* they told Yuri, and when they finally got up close to him, and it got to be *their turn* to get his autograph, a reporter was yelling a question but The Magician didn't even look at the reporter—

"He just looked at us," one of the boys shouted. "And he said, 'You are the Soviet team, the Champions!' And then he said, 'Goodness, you must all be very, very good!'"

"And he kept speaking to us and smiling to us!" said another boy. "He was very friendly!"

"And we told him about you, Yuri! We told him you were the greatest player of all of us, the greatest Youth player in the Soviet Union and he listened closely, and the reporters kept yelling out questions at him the whole time, but he ignored them and listened only to *us!*"

'Only to us!' shouted another boy.

"And they were important reporters, too!" said yet

another boy. "They had important positions!"

"And then The Magician asked us what was wrong with you, and we told him you had the flu!" said another boy. "And the reporters kept yelling questions at him, loud questions, but he just kept listening to us!"

"And then he took his pen, and wrote this to you, Yuri, look!" And then the boy stepped forward and presented Yuri with the big surprise that they had all brought back for him from Stockholm—a large glossy photograph of *The American Magician* in his beautiful red, white, and blue uniform—the white with the red and blue trim. Yuri took the picture in his hand and stared down at it—his entire body flushing warm and weightless, his eyes beginning to water. Written across was:

My very best wishes to you Yuri
Tommy Haasen

Yuri couldn't understand the words, but the boys told him what it said; they had it memorized. One of the boys told Yuri that it was the same photo that had been on the cover of a famous American sports magazine.

"What's wrong?" one of the boys asked.

Yuri wiped his hand across his eyes and shook his head.

"Don't you like it?" asked another.

Yuri nodded several times, brushing his hand across again. It would become his most cherished possession—the color photograph of The American Magician with the personalized inscription and autograph. On his return to Letegorsk, he would put it up over his bed, right between Trotsky and Kharlamov. It wasn't a large poster size like theirs, but it would be the most special. Over his bed now he would have the greatest of the Soviets and the greatest, not only of the Americans, but in the world.

The greatest of all time.

Over the next couple years, Yuri led his Letegorsk team to undefeated seasons, and his skills developed even further—far beyond the proportion of the other boys. At sixteen, he was selected as a member of the Soviet Union's Junior Red Army team, and once again moved to Moscow. He became a starting forward for the Junior Reds and during that season took full advantage of all the faculties and facilities available at the Red Army Sports School. Yuri found the School to be a fascinating place, learning that even the senior players on the Red Army teams studied regularly, even after earning degrees. It was taught at the School that hockey was a game of creativity and precision, and that it was practiced best by players who were developed not only physically, but mentally and spiritually as well. Signs, which alluded to sentiments such as this, frequented the walls and doorways of the campus. One in particular, which hung along the wall in the study center, said something to the effect that: "If a player ceases to develop intellectually, if his curiosity is dulled and the circle of his interests diminishes to the size of a puck, then inevitably his mastery of the sport will also cease to grow. The practice of any sport, including hockey, is a creative exercise. And creativity is only for the curious."

Yuri learned to discipline himself in academics, just as

the quote suggested, and also learned to incorporate them into his game, learning that it was all *one* experience—all a part of the whole.

It was exciting for Yuri—the whole concept and experience of the School; but it was still the nights that he most looked forward to, when he would go down to the film room to run the reels of the USA team, studying with endless fascination, the intricate movements of the free flowing red, white, and blue—the movements of *The American Magician*. The Magician had since been drafted by the Detroit Red Wings, and so Yuri searched the school for Red Wings films—he searched for every film he could find. Yuri studied every film the Sports School had of The Magician, studying them night after night, watching them over and over and over, scrutinizing every movement, every shift, every deke, every stride—running and re-running and reversing in slow motion, stopping and starting—examining everything down to its finest, most intricate detail, searching to find in himself the same instincts and rhythms that The Magician had.

As before, the more Yuri studied the great player, the more obvious it became to him that even those who called him the greatest in the world had no idea how great he truly was. Others saw the sensational moves and the miraculous plays, but they did not see the motor that was creating it— the life—which was where the magic really was. The Magician was *above* the *flow*. He was above all other movements. He was seamless, edgeless; he felt *everything* on the ice—not just himself and his line mates but the opposition as well. He was truly *mystical,* truly *magical.* Yuri even swore at times—sometimes in the wee-hours of night, while sitting alone in the dim lamplight of the film room—that he could see a faint *glow* surrounding The Magician. It was like a radiating light that seemed to protect him and encase him, rendering him nearly untouchable. Sometimes Yuri even stood and walked towards the screen, his shirttails hanging out in a staggering weariness, to touch the canvas with his hand, and then to rub his eyes—reminding himself of his lack of sleep, but at the same time swearing to himself that he could see it... that he could actually *see it*... It was like a *glow*. . . It was like a strange sort of white light.

Yuri began to see himself in dreams—the same dreams as The Magician. He dreamed of mastering The Magician's movements and of one day stepping onto the same sheet of ice with him, and of countering those movements and of entering the same *flow*. The dream became a focus for Yuri, and soon became his goal. The goal became an obsession, and the obsession gave him new life, new fuel. He would work harder than ever before. He would work and study feverishly hard, with the hopes of one day earning a position on one of the senior Soviet teams that would maybe one day—in eight or ten years, when he was developed enough—play the Americans and give him the opportunity to step onto the same sheet of ice as the greatest of all time.

But it was during this season, during this time in Moscow—when Yuri Kershy was setting his sights and honing his focus on the movements of the greatest player in the world—in the hopes of one day facing him, of entering the same *flow*—that news broke out that The Magician was done.

Finished.

The stories ran rampant through Moscow, circulating in the streets and markets—the newspapers saying that

The American Magician—Tommy Haasen—had probably committed suicide, but that the Americans were not saying. Scandalous rumors flooded the city, most of them saying that The Magician had been corrupted by the huge sums of money he was being paid, and that he had staged a death and then fled with the money to Mexico or to Argentina.

Yuri's heart broke. He did not believe the stories. The people who told those stories and passed those rumors did not know The Magician. They did not understand him. They did not know that a person as extraordinary—as *special*—as Tommy Haasen, would never allow something so trivial as money to ruin him. It was an enigma to Yuri what had happened, but he knew that whatever it was, that it had to have been something colossal. Something extreme. It would take something catastrophically horrible to topple a person as great as The American Magician.

Yuri descended into severe depression. His dream was shattered, his focus gone. His spirits spiraled downward, taking him into a stage of his life where he lost interest in nearly everything. Nothing held importance anymore, and anything that was brought to his attention, he either dismissed or questioned—wondering what it was all about, what it all meant, what it was all for? He questioned the meaning of life, the meaning of existence. His studies faltered, except for philosophy, which he read for several hours daily, and for the remainder of the playing season his game was not up to standard. The Junior Reds won an International tournament late in the year in Garmisch-Partenkirchen West Germany, and Yuri was named star of the tournament, and was also later named *Junior Sportsman of the Year* in the U.S.S.R. But he did not care. His eyes continued to twinkle, but in a downcast silence. He spoke to no one about his trauma because no one understood. He spoke of it only to his mother, who as always, continued to listen and continued to console.

The period of Yuri's depression lasted for nearly a year, but was then finally alleviated somewhat, when during the following season, to Yuri's utter *astonishment,* he was moved up to join the senior squad's roster, and at age seventeen became the youngest forward ever to join the Central Red Army hockey team.

Yuri's heart was suddenly pumping again—pumping with adrenaline twenty-four hours a day. It was like living in a *dream*—an unbelievable *dream!* He was now skating *in the Palace! In Moscow!* Skating on the same ice—on the *very same team*—as his childhood hero, Gvesik Trotsky, and the great Sergei Mikilov!

When the news of this promotion hit the remote little village of Letegorsk, it sparked a revel of excitement and celebration in the community that it had never before known. The little village was suddenly basking in a whole new glow of pride and glory—a glory that exceeded anything and everything of its kind from prior years. *Their boy—their very own hometown hero, Yuri Kershy—* who they had all nurtured and supported over the years, was now wearing the brilliant red, blue, and gold of the greatest team on earth: the colors of the illustrious Central Red Army of the U.S.S.R.

But it was after only two weeks of living the dream, of

skating with the most prestigious, most elite team in the land, that Yuri's astonishment—and the glow in Letegorsk—turned to *shock,* when one morning before practice, Coach Sokolov asked Yuri to join Trotsky and Mikilov, to experiment as the Red Army's new starting front line.

Yuri's heart jolted. It was suddenly pounding hard in his chest, his eyes blinking, looking nervously at Coach Sokolov. He was confused—bewildered—his head swimmy and light—he did not understand. He certainly did not expect to even play on the second line, or even the third; he thought surely he would only be a reliever for a while and ride the bench and learn from the others over a course of time, for several years even—*but to play with Trotsky and Mikilov?* That was the left wing position, the position of the late, great Valeri Kharlamov, the greatest Soviet player of all time—whose picture still hung over Yuri's bed in Letegorsk! Yuri's knees went weak, his mouth dry. His heart pounded like thunder in his chest, out of control. He did not know what Coach Sokolov could possibly be thinking. He did not understand how anyone could possibly think that *he,* Yuri Kershy, was capable of playing with *such greats.* Surely Coach Sokolov was mistaken in his thinking. Trotsky and Mikilov were like living *Soviet icons.* They were *the leaders of the Red Army*—the greatest team in the nation, the greatest in the world. They were like Gods, the legends of the land, and *he* was only Yuri Kershy from the little town of Letegorsk!

On the announcement of this new arrangement however, Trotsky and Mikilov regarded Yuri with kindness. They were cordial and polite to him, and spoke personally to him, and revealed little other emotion.

But Yuri was speechless. He was terrified. He swallowed deeply, his eyes blinking, his heart pumping the breath out of him. He stood at the face-off on his left wing, looking at his childhood hero, Gvesik Trotsky at center ice—*the Great Gvesik Trotsky*—the same Gvesik Trotsky that still hung over his bed in Letegorsk, one of the greatest legends of all time; and beyond him, over on the right flank, the famous *Blue-eyed Comet,* Sergei Mikilov—both looking at him as they waited for the others to line up, and for the dropping of the puck. Yuri was standing at the left wing position, the very same spot that the late great Valeri Kharlamov held, the three of them—Trotsky, Kharlamov and Mikilov—known as the *Red Express,* the greatest front line in Soviet history. Yuri's knees trembled terribly—his mouth dry, trying to swallow, trying to focus. He couldn't breathe. He thought surely he wouldn't be able to even skate—surely he would never last the shift—he just wouldn't be able to do it—certainly not the workout—and Coach Sokolov would soon take him to the side and call an end to this preposterous experiment.

But as the puck dropped, Yuri found himself suddenly sprung into motion—an instantaneous super-speed action—his movement generated by some instinctive inner motor that propelled him into a syncopated pace so horrendously intense that he nearly lost all sense of conscious self—other than a desperate struggle to survive—becoming completely engulfed in the ricocheting, heart-pounding whirlwind—the puck on his stick, then a connecting pass to Trotsky, but *into his skates*—Trotsky coughing it up onto his stick without breaking stride—*brilliant*—

embarrassing—the puck on his stick again, a snap pass across to Mikilov, but *into his skates again—* Mikilov carving into it picking it up perfectly—*brilliant—* embarrassing—the only feeling close to a conscious thought being that he could not do this—he could not make it into the next second—that he could not keep up—that he couldn't last—he couldn't hang on—it was all too fast—he just couldn't do it—he couldn't make it...

But he did.

He survived—not only the next second, but the duration of the shift.

And the workout. And the remainder of that first day's practice.

As he did the next.

And the next.

And as that week came to a close, Yuri found himself gathering his things with the others as the Central Red Army prepared to depart for a four series road trip, beginning with a game way out east in Siberia against the mighty Traktor of Chelyabinsk.

The arena in Chelyabinsk was packed to the ceiling and loud, full of fur hats and gold teeth, vodka and cigarettes, and again Yuri grew nervous. He was scared. He'd never been in an arena that was brimming with this kind of noise and raucous energy. Before the game, in the locker room, Coach Sokolov announced that the Red Army would be starting with its new front line of Trotsky, Mikilov and Kershy—to which Yuri's body responded by shutting down. He couldn't breathe. Every fiber in his body was shaking like a leaf in the wind, and when the puck finally dropped and the game began, Yuri found himself catapulted into another high-speed roller coaster ride—a whipping, whirling vortex of near out of control pace and intensity—so insanely fast, that he could not concentrate, focus or follow. The Traktor starters were lightening quick, they were everywhere, all over the ice, buzzing with overwhelming speed and precision. But Yuri noticed that Trotsky and Mikilov were also faster—significantly faster—almost completely different than in practice *they were flying*—yet smooth as silk—the Blue-eyed Comet streaking up the boards in a high-speed drift, deking the Traktor defensemen and streaming in on goal—*firing* a blistering rocket—and then the three of them suddenly arcing back out of the zone, high-tailing it back up the ice as the mighty Traktors attacked back against them in a lightening blitzkrieg of overwhelming power and speed, buzzing into the zone, firing fast and relentless on the Red Army goal, the *Siberian crowd roaring* and *roaring* and *roaring*. Yuri could not concentrate. Everything was whipping and whirling, feeling like a desperate life or death struggle, all the way through to the end, and then with only a minute remaining and the score tied and the Traktors firing hard and fast, shot after shot, and Yuri feeling defeat coming on, Trotsky and Mikilov suddenly broke out of the zone, rushing the length of the ice, attacking into the Traktor end, firing two quick shots and missing, and then Yuri, by some means unbeknownst to him, tipped a set-up pass back to Mikilov who unleashed a blistering rocket from the top of the right circle, catching the upper corner of the net—scoring for the Red Army, and putting away the threatening Traktor of Chelyabinsk.

Yuri trembled. Even after the game. He had never in his life experienced anything like it, anything so fast, so harrowing, so *loud*. It was *unbelievably fast*. And Trotsky and Mikilov, *they were so unbelievably fast too!* Yuri couldn't believe it was even *them*—the same two whom he had been skating with all of that previous week. Both of them always put out a hundred percent in practice, it wasn't that they had been holding back, it was more like they had become completely different people in Chelyabinsk. Yuri had always played the same in practice as he had in games, but now he had seen what it was to focus and prepare, and then to *peak* for a performance. *That's what Trotsky and Mikilov had done.* It also began to dawn on Yuri, just how great Trotsky and Mikilov really were, and how he, Yuri Kershy had absolutely no business playing with them.

And it wasn't only Trotsky and Mikilov, it was *all of them*—*all* the Red Army players, and the Traktor players too.

Yuri felt certain now—without question—that he was in over his head. He decided he would tell Coach Sokolov, and ask to be taken out and just be a reliever. Maybe Coach Sokolov had already decided this on his own, as he, Yuri Kershy, had played very poorly, and had certainly let the Red Army down. But to be sure—and to acknowledge his own inadequacies—Yuri decided to approach Coach Sokolov on his own accord.

Which he did—after the game in the locker room.

And then again in the lobby of the hotel.

Twice in the hotel.

But Coach Sokolov was always too busy talking to the

other players, and would hardly look at him. Yuri would stand patiently alongside, waiting for a chance, and then would clear his throat slightly to speak, but then Coach Sokolov wouldn't even notice him; he would just go on talking to the other players and to the other coaches and would hardly pay any attention to him. Yuri didn't know what to do. Coach Sokolov never said a word to him, never even looked at him, or even acknowledged him. It was as if he, Yuri Kershy, wasn't even on the team.

The next game was just a partial trip back, to the city of Gorki, where they were to play the Torpedo team, and Yuri thought that maybe it would not be as demanding— as the Torpedoes were having a poor season and were way down in the standings.

But again it was a devastating experience—sixty minutes of non-stop, super-speed, high intensity struggle, and again Yuri felt himself overwhelmed, caught up in a spinning, whipping confusion—the Torpedoes streaking up and down the ice, firing shots upon shots at the Red Army goal, the Gorki crowd rallying in a wild feverous roar—and again Yuri felt the Red Army about to fall to defeat when miraculously in the final minutes, they were again saved by two back to back rockets of Mikilov's, allowing them to luckily squeak past by a score of 4-3.

From Gorki, they traveled further west—all the way to the west coast—to Latvia, to the port city of Riga, where they would engage the famed Dynamos. It was a three-hour flight, most of which Yuri sat through nervously, his stomach tight, pondering endlessly over his disappointing performances in Siberia and Gorki. He thought for a moment that maybe they just played a faster game in Siberia—but then considered that Dynamo Riga was in second place in the National Elite League, and so they would surely be just as fast, and probably be even faster. Yuri looked around at the other players on the plane to see if they were showing any signs of nervousness or worry, but they were all sitting calmly, reading or playing chess or sleeping. Sitting next to Yuri, in the aisle seat, was Mikilov, and in the aisle seat across from him was Trotsky. Both Mikilov and Trotsky were doing the same as they had done on the trip out—Trotsky put glasses on and read, and Mikilov sat perfectly still, just staring at the seatback in front of him. Mikilov was a very deep person, Yuri was beginning to find out. Only seldomly throughout the flight would Trotsky and Mikilov exchange words, and when they did, it was always in low voices, inaudible to Yuri. They said very little to him, and so he just looked out his window, peering down at the expansive land far below—snow-blown Russia, cold, vast and barren, stretching all that great distance from Siberia all the way to Latvia.

Yuri suddenly felt a welling coming into his eyes... He closed them... then closed them tighter, but it kept coming. He put his palm up to his eyes, brushing it across and then pressed back but it wouldn't stop. He couldn't do that, he just couldn't. He was not a child any longer. Not anymore. He was no longer—

Suddenly it occurred to Yuri, as if someone had flicked on a light, just *what it was* that he had become. He recalled Coach Sokolov's words from a lecture he had once given to the Junior Reds—and recalled similar speeches given by other coaches while he was with the

Youth All Stars—about how hockey was a thumbnail synopsis of the Soviet ideal. It was referred to as the Soviet political model in action—the Communist system in a crucible, for all the world to witness: five players operating in full cooperation—in full harmony—for the strength and good of the whole. It was a living example of its superiority over the individualistic Capitalist systems of the West—which operated with five players who were not as fully connected, or even necessarily committed, but rather played as five independents with individual motifs, attempting to merely function together as a unit in order to achieve an end result. Yuri recalled Coach Sokolov trying to clarify his point by making the example of playing a piano—pointing out that the Soviet system was five fingers all connected to the same hand with a single intent, fit and able to make music, whereas the Western system was five individuals all contributing to the piece with a single finger of their own, trying to accomplish the same result. He explained that this was why Soviet hockey was so important, not only for the Soviet Union to witness as a nation, but for the World to see as a whole—that it was a working portrait, a working example of the effectiveness of the Communist system—of *Marxist-Leninism*—and that the Red Army players were the premiere carriers and exhibitors of this example—and that as youths, the aspiration to become one of these select players, to become one of these special people, was one of the highest and loftiest aims in the land.

Yuri's heart was suddenly pounding fast again... He was *one of them.* He had become *one of the carriers, one of the exhibitors.* He had become a part of *the crucible—and all eyes were on him, the entire nation watching him, looking for inspiration, looking for direction, looking for validation of their way of life, depending on him.* Yuri suddenly felt frightfully warm—the world was tipping upside down on him, that vast expansive land far below, the entire nation of the Soviet Union was suddenly on top of him, on top of his shoulders, all that great, massive weight crushing him, the responsibility overwhelming him—he couldn't do it, he couldn't take it, he had to get out—

Yuri suddenly jerked upward slightly as if awaking from a nightmare. He wiped his eyes again, then turned, looking to the aisle—

And suddenly he was looking at a pretty young maiden. An apple girl. She smiled at Yuri, and Yuri quickly ran a hand over his hair and then his eyes and told her that he did not care for one, or for any crackers. The apple girl started to say something but then stopped and cleared her throat, touching her free hand lightly to her neck and smiling; then she started again. She said to Yuri that none of the hockey teams hardly ever took apples. Yuri looked at the apples; they were suspended from her arm in a beautiful basket with a pretty red checkered cloth inside, all shiny and green and perfectly arranged. Yuri suddenly felt sad for the maiden, and so he told her he would take one. She picked one out for him and handed it across and then remained alongside, to visit briefly—speaking to Yuri over Mikilov's unwavering stare. Mikilov had also refused an apple, but Yuri had not noticed how it was done. He thought that maybe the communication was done in a subtle manner, or maybe the apple girl knew

Mikilov from other flights and maybe knew that he never took any. Yuri kept referring to the maiden in his mind as the "apple girl"—that's what they had called them when he was jetting around the country with the Junior Reds. They were on all the Aeroflot flights. The *apple girls*. And then on arrival, it was the *flower girls*. Most of them—both the apple girls and the flower girls—were usually quite pretty, and always very friendly.

The apple girl was saying to Yuri that the hockey teams took very few apples, whereas the regular public was absolutely ravenous over them. Yuri told the apple girl that most of the players probably just had a lot on their minds, and to this, the apple girl smiled and said that she thought they must just *have it very good* in the National Elite League, especially being on the Central Red Army team. Yuri smiled back, not replying to that comment, but he had wanted to—he had wanted to tell her that it was maybe good for the rest of them, but for him it was *terrifying!*

The apple girl continued up the aisle and Yuri looked back out his window. Then suddenly it dawned on him that she had known his name. *How did she know that?* Everybody knew Trotsky and Mikilov, they were famous, they were stars, known everywhere, but how would this stewardess, this apple girl, on an Aeroflot flight from Gorki to Riga, know *him?* Yuri looked up and saw the apple girl near the front of the plane speaking to two other stewardesses in the aisle, and the other two were looking back at him and smiling as she spoke. Yuri looked back out his window at the land again far below. He suddenly felt funny. It was like a nervousness, but not the kind of nervousness he had been feeling a few minutes ago; this was a different kind, a kind he'd never experienced before.

A short while later the apple girl returned, this time with a sterling teapot—offering tea and cookies. She stood alongside again, looking past Mikilov to Yuri. Yuri smiled at her and she blushed and touched her hand to her collar and then glanced up at her friends who were serving tea up at the front, their eyes watching. She held the cookies in a pretty arrangement on the serving tray and told Yuri that none of the players ever took cookies either—several took tea, but hardly ever cookies.

Again, Yuri felt sad for the maiden and her job. He told her that he would like one, and when she handed it to him, he noticed her glance with a smile again to her friends up at the front of the plane.

But this new nervousness plagued Yuri, to the point that he found it difficult to speak to this girl—which he did not understand. He had wanted to ask the maiden her name and where she was from but somehow, mysteriously, he could not find the courage. Why? She wasn't like Coach Sokolov, or some revered person of authority—which, understandably, generated some natural nervousness. This was an apple girl, a stewardess, on an Aeroflot flight from Gorki to Riga. The apple girl was now telling Yuri that she and her cousin Oxanna had tickets for the Red Army game against Dynamo next week in Moscow, and that they would both be there, at the Palace, to see him play. Yuri had wanted to tell the maiden that he would certainly not be skating in next week's game because by that time—when the Red Army returned to Moscow—he would most certainly be relegated to a reliever.

Yuri watched the maiden as she moved onward again, serving and offering from side to side. She looked perfect... in her navy blue skirt and white short-sleeved blouse that all the Aeroflot stewardesses wore. Yuri noticed the red and blue trim along her collar, the glossy red belt strapped thinly around her waist... the soft skin of her arm, her smooth, silky hair as she reached across under a reading light.

Suddenly Yuri was struck again by what the maiden had just said to him... Actually, it was *the way* she had said it. She said that she and her cousin would be at the Palace to, *'see you play'*... And it wasn't like, to see *you, the Red Army*... it was more like, to see *you, Yuri Kershy... What was going on?*

As the Red Army de-boarded the plane in Riga, they walked across the tarmac from the flight stairs to the coach bus that was waiting to take them to the hotel—all wearing their navy blue greatcoats with the gold, double-breasted buttons, and the red and gold shoulder epaulets. The pavement was wet and snowy, and darkness was coming on fast, and the flower girls stood along the path holding their colorful bouquets—all seeming to be looking at Yuri. *Why were they all looking at him?*

Yuri searched for the pretty maiden but was unable to spot her. Then suddenly she was walking alongside him. She wore a navy blue Aeroflot coat similar to the Red Army greatcoats. Yuri had never noticed that before. They looked the same. She placed a single flower into the upper button hole of Yuri's lapel, and then she took Yuri's hand and placed something in it, closing his hand over it with her own. Then she stepped back and away from Yuri, joining the other stewardesses to the side. As Yuri boarded the bus he turned to look back at her again—to which she raised her hand slightly in a wave, which Yuri returned with a slight wave of his own.

Yuri kept his hand closed, watching the maiden on the tarmac through the window of the bus until they had departed the airport. When Yuri opened his palm, he found a piece of paper, which he carefully unfolded. It said: Uta Kalineslev. Then an address and a telephone number. It was a Moscow address. She was from Moscow!

The game in Riga was another nightmare for Yuri. The Dynamos seemed to completely dominate the ice— they were everywhere—attacking like buzzing bees, swarming them, pressuring them to death. Yuri had never seen anything so quick, so sudden, so instantaneously fast in his entire life, even in his wildest imagination. All he could see was yellow and blue, the Dynamo colors, swirling him, attacking him. Again, he could not concentrate, could not anticipate, could not focus or respond right—it was all too fast. The Dynamos were like lightening, they were super-humans, they were everywhere, and again Yuri was flustered and overwhelmed, and to him, it was *pure luck* that they were saved from defeat and got out of Latvia with a very fortunate 3-3 tie.

Again Yuri trembled. He could not take it any longer. He did not know what to do. He could not understand Coach Sokolov wanting him to fumble up and weigh down the Red Army, especially with players like Trotsky and Mikilov. Yuri was all nerves. He could not eat or sleep, he could not even think straight anymore—he had become a conduit of fear, a constant bundle of trembling nerves. He wrote to his mother and told her that he did not think he could go on any longer, and that he was in over his head—that the National Elite League was just too fast for him, and that all the players—every one of them—were *superstars,* and that it was super-sonic fast, and that it was nothing even remotely close to what it looked like from the seats or on television.

The final road game was in the Ukraine against Kiev, and again the Red Army barely slipped past, by a score of 2-1, and again Yuri suffered.

On the return flight to Moscow, Yuri again tried to approach Coach Sokolov, but again Coach Sokolov ignored him. On returning to Moscow, they would once again face Dynamo Riga, hosting them at the Palace, and Yuri felt certain that this time they would not be able to hold them off. The Dynamos were in second place in the League, right behind the Central Red Army, and Yuri felt certain that the Dynamos were surely the stronger club and would now knock them out—unless Coach Sokolov came to his senses!

Yuri scrambled his mind for a way out, for some form of refuge. He remained in his seat throughout the flight, dazed and benumbed, his eyes peering out the window and shifting around the cabin. It bewildered him how the rest of the team seemed to remain so serene, so focused, and how he, Yuri Kershy, seemed to be the only one who was struggling, the only one petrified, the only one suffering. Yuri thought of the training they had gone through at the Sports School, when the psychologists had led them through the meditation exercises, where they would relax themselves and elevate themselves, allowing themselves to feel a connection with the others—to feel the movements and inclinations of others, putting their deductive minds to rest—as its work was done—allowing everything to be given to the serene calm of the creative right brain which would take over and guide them on a higher plane. Yuri had never thought about the exercises much before, other than when they did them at the Sports School. He had never seriously applied them on the ice, and certainly not in a game situation. He had never really understood the need to. But maybe... *maybe that's why Trotsky and Mikilov became so quiet on game days... so internal...*

In Moscow, the people packed the Palace, waiting for the return of their hometown team, the Central Red Army. The noise and energy in the building were at an all-time high and the power of the crowd could be felt through the locker room walls and the ceiling above as the Red Army prepared themselves for the game. As they dressed, Yuri said nervously to the player next to him, *'It's going to be loud, like Chelyabinsk,'* to which the experienced comrade calmly responded: *'Chelyabinsk wasn't loud, Yuri. Tonight you'll hear loud.'* Yuri took a couple breaths in response to this, and swallowed deeply. Then the player added, that when they charge out of the tunnel tonight to take the ice, *'It's going to be a glorious one... so hang on to yourself. Keep your focus.'*

As the team finished dressing, the conversations and banter gradually subsided. The players began taking their places on the locker room benches, waiting for Coach

Sokolov's instructions and words. The only remaining activity was that of the trainers taping and addressing a couple player's injuries. Coach Sokolov began pacing slowly in front of the team, blue suit and red tie, hands behind his back, bringing the room to a complete stillness, leaving only the enormity of energy brewing through the walls and the ceiling above. He began by telling the team that the Palace was beyond capacity that evening—not only sold out, but that officials had sold thousands of extra tickets allowing spectators to sit in the aisles and stand in the corridors. He told them that the game was being broadcast live on television and radio across the entire Soviet Union, that it would be one of the highest viewed games of year—and that the reason for all of this was because Dynamo Riga had come to Moscow to knock out the Red Army and that millions of people all across the nation would be watching, looking to the Red Army as the defenders of the land, as the protectors of their ideals, as the essence of everything they held dear—and that not only would the Red Army have to defend the Palace, but they must emerge decisively victorious, and leave the Dynamo in crushing defeat.

Yuri knew this to be true. His mother had told him that she and all her friends, the townswomen, would be cooking at the Letegorsk community center that night with several televisions set up—where everyone would be gathering—to watch the game. According to his mother, it was going to be a big event.

Yuri looked nervously to the player next to him, at his shoulder, at the big blue star with the golden hammer and sickle at the center. He looked up at his glossy red helmet with the national insignia on the side, then glanced downwards at the player's elite red breezers with the broad blue stripe and the big gold stars running down. Yuri looked down at his own breezers, and his heart began to pound. He was wearing the same uniform—the uniform of the greatest team in the land. How had he gotten here? He looked to the player on the other side of him—Trotsky—who was staring downwards taking quick, hyper breaths, as if preparing himself for a deep dive. Yuri looked at the players across and they were doing the same—eyes focused, preparing themselves for battle, listening to Coach Sokolov as he paced between them. Yuri tried to swallow but couldn't, his mouth was too dry. The others seemed to be *all business* and *he*, Yuri Kershy, was *all nerves*. Everybody's eyes were focused and concentrated, and his own eyes were darting around the room like a frightened puppy.

Yuri didn't know how he had gotten himself into this, but he was clear about one thing: he certainly knew that he did not belong. And it was also very clear to him just exactly *who he was* and *where he was*... He was a boy amongst men. And these were not just ordinary men, these were *great men*. Men who were about to go into battle. Men who had defended the Palace many times, and had defeated well beyond. Men who had toured Europe victoriously, and the great cities of the world, including North America where they had engaged the famed millionaires of the NHL—who played a violent, hard checking game—but had defeated them as well, on their own soil.

Yes, in this locker room were not only some of the finest players in the Soviet Union, but some of the best in the world—and he, Yuri Kershy, from the little town of

Letegorsk, was somehow in amongst them. He was trapped. And he couldn't get out. He couldn't just hold up his hand now and ask to be dismissed—he had foiled his chances at that. He would have to charge through the tunnel and into the arena with 20,000 Muscovites waiting for them, expecting so much, with the entire nation of millions watching on television or listening to their radios.

Yuri noticed a change in the crowd through the walls... Music had started playing. Coach Sokolov had noticed it too, because he paused... Then he said, *They've taken the ice.*

Yuri thought he was going to faint.

They're out there waiting for us.

Coach Sokolov's words were fading in and out and he, Yuri, was now hyper-ventilating, just like Trotsky, except his own was involuntary, out of sheer fear. He wanted to run. He wanted to go home and stay with his mother. He had told his mother about his fears and troubles but she had responded by telling him to just keep going. *Just keep following the path, Yuri,* she had said, *and do your best, and things will work out. You'll see.*

His mother's advice was advice for a boy. She did not understand that he was now amongst *men.* Yuri thought of Uta Kalineslev. He wanted to ring her up at her flat and invite her for a walk. They could ride the Metro down to the Arbat where they would stroll the sidewalks, listen to the musicians and watch the street artists and maybe he would buy her some ice cream.

But she was out there too, in that teeming crowd, brimming with anticipation, expecting him to defend the Palace, defend the honor of the Central Red Army.

Yuri thought of the American Magician, Tommy

Haasen—of his magical movements—and of his own silly dreams that he had had, of trying to find the same magic within himself.

Childhood dreams.

Or more like *childish* dreams. Dreams of a boy.

And that's exactly what he was: *a boy.*

But there was no turning back now. He would have to charge through the tunnel and face the Dynamo—the famed Dynamo that he had barely survived in Riga—those super-fast, super-human skaters that were so difficult to shake...

Suddenly, something occurred to Yuri... They had double-manned him in Riga... The Dynamo had covered him on the back check with both their right winger and center, from the deep blue line, all the way into the Dynamo end... Why had they done that? And why was this just occurring to him now? Probably because he was accustomed to being double covered—he had experienced it throughout his entire career—ever since he was a young boy in Letegorsk, it was as natural to him as the game itself. But why would they double man him in the National Elite League? He was a *new player,* a mere rookie—and one not even fit to play amongst such greats. The one advantage of being double-covered of course, was that it always left at least one of his mates open—or two of them partially open—which was why he often had as many assists as goals, which, to him, was essentially why his scoring averages were often so high.

Coach Sokolov was saying that goaltender *Nemynkyna* would lead them onto the ice, followed by *Trotsky, Mikilov and Kershy*, and then—

Wait! What? Yuri had heard his name—Coach Sokolov

had said it in front of the entire team—*What? He* would be leading the Red Army into the Palace? On the road they had followed goaltender Nemynkyna into the arenas in whatever order they happened to assemble in, but this was obviously different. This was special. A specific order. Coach Sokolov wanted this entrance orchestrated; he wanted to make a statement. But with *him,* Yuri Kershy, a mere rookie—leading the Red Army into the Palace?

All of them were standing now, taking their places, and Yuri found himself moving towards the door. Trotsky patted Yuri's shoulder pad and then Mikilov's glove patted his other shoulder as he stepped in front of Yuri, taking his place directly behind Trotsky. Yuri's legs trembled. He did not think he could make it out of the locker room, let alone through the tunnel...

As they settled to a ready, Coach Sokolov gave his final words, standing amongst them: *"Keep clearly at the back of your minds who you are, what you represent, and the honor that you must defend. Keep at the forefront of your minds the fundamentals of the game, everything we've worked on and dwelled upon. Pay close attention to each other. And give it everything you've got... Everything. Do this... and there is no question what the outcome of this game is going to be."*

They stood in stillness, digesting Coach Sokolov's words, the heavy drone of the crowd permeating the walls and ceiling above.

Then Coach Sokolov said: *"Ready?"* He said this before every game, at the conclusion of his speech: *Ready?. .*

Then a long pause would follow, during which, the players seemed to focus like lasers, hyping themselves to go—and during which, Yuri trembled like a cornered deer.

Then after that lengthy pause, that final period in which players collected themselves, Coach Sokolov would lower his tone and simply say, *"Alright, let's go"*—after which, the locker room doors immediately blew open and the Red Army began filing out.

As Yuri found himself moving through the locker room doors and into the hallway, he felt another glove from behind, jostle his shoulder pad, *"Show them what you've got, Yuri,"* said the voice. It was defenseman Lentylov—the top defenseman in the league. He said it in a raised voice, adjusting to the growing noise as they moved into the hallway. They were all so good to him, Yuri thought, all so supportive. They truly were comrades.

But Yuri was terrified. They were moving at a brisk pace down the hallway, moving towards the security police who stood up ahead where they would turn into the tunnel. As they made the turn, the noise and energy of the crowd grew louder, increasing significantly with every step. Yuri looked ahead, beyond Mikilov, Trotsky and Nemynkyna to the light at the end of the tunnel—at the brightness of the arena where he could see the Dynamo players skating past in their bright yellow jerseys, their blue breezers and glossy blue helmets. Then Nemynkyna started into a trot, as did the rest of them, quickening their clip, their skates prancing down the rubber tunnel flooring, the brightness of the arena looming larger and the noise level growing heavier—and then Nemynkyna broke into a run as did the rest of them in sequence, charging the last five or six steps out of the tunnel and onto the Palace ice.

And suddenly there was an *eruption*, a spontaneous combustible roar that burst open like a cannon shot, and as it did, they were simultaneously hit by a heavy wave of pressurized air as if someone had turned a blast furnace onto them—except the wave wasn't temperature, it was *volume.* Yuri had never felt or heard anything like it, but he was skating through it, his eyes focused ahead on Mikilov—on Mikilov's hair protruding out the lower back of his helmet, his neck and his name just above his jersey number. Yuri kept his eyes there and only there, remembering his comrades words, *It's going to be glorious... so hang onto yourself. Keep your focus.*

Yuri had never experienced anything like this. He could feel the volume in his chest. It reminded him of the first time he'd heard a live rock and roll band. The band had come to Letegorsk to play for a teen dance at the community center and Yuri recalled the sensation of the electric bass guitar—of its volume thumping in his chest.

Yuri shifted his eyes slightly—they were out to mid ice now, crossing the red line. He glanced up, and around, at the surrounding waves of humanity—clamoring on their feet, expressing themselves at the top of their lungs, many waving flags, large, silky red flags and banners wavering them from side to side.

As they reached the far end of the rink and went into their arc, Yuri looked back to the far end of the arena, to the tunnel from which they had emerged... The silky red flags were there too. They were everywhere, all the way around. Yuri looked upwards, and they were there too, all the way up into the darkness of the upper decks, thousands of them. It was a wondrous sight and a frightening feeling, yet exhilarating. "My goodness," Yuri said to himself, saying it out loud—then suddenly realizing that he couldn't even hear himself, not even inside his own head. And with that, something dawned upon Yuri. During practices, during inner team scrimmages, Coach Sokolov often made the entire team wear earplugs. Yuri had thought the exercise to be brilliant, as obviously, they were meant to hone their skills without sound, to heighten their other senses. But it had never occurred to Yuri that another reason Coach Sokolov did this was to prepare them to play under deafening conditions—which they would certainly be experiencing tonight, especially during Red Army attacks.

The Reds circled with the Dynamos, then split apart into their respective ends of the rink. As Yuri ran his warm-up drills with Trotsky and Mikilov, he glanced repeatedly over his shoulder—just as he had done in Siberia and Latvia and in the Ukraine—at the Dynamos at the other end, seeing their numbers and remembering some of them, those fast ones, those superhuman ones. Yuri looked at Trotsky and Mikilov and noticed that they—as before—were not looking. None of the others looked. Their faces were all focused and serene, and again Yuri felt out of place, out of sync—just as he had in Siberia and in Latvia, and on the plane. He looked at the Dynamos again, and once again thought of the meditations...

And it was then, that Yuri, like his teammates, turned away from the Dynamos. He put his back to them and began an effort to focus inward, telling himself that he *must now prepare*. Instead of feeling fear and nerves, he must now find his inner self, his center—he must feel a connection with everything around him—just as the meditations went. His skills and abilities were honed and ready, and he must now turn them over to a higher plane, a *truer* plane...

... And allow it to take over.

The Moscow crowd witnessed a fast-paced shoulder to shoulder contest that evening—a super-speed human chess game of seamless back and forth, end to end action—the Dynamo Riga pressing a constant relentless threat against the Central Red Army until mid-way through the second period when it started to happen. That's when the transformation began to become visible—right before the people's eyes, the people of Moscow and the millions of others watching on television all across the country—of Trotsky, Mikilov and Kershy as *excellence* began to transform itself into *greatness*—as they began to *gel*—as they began to spark— networking cleaner, sharper, clearer— bonding, becoming one—beginning to click into a lightening rapport, beginning to weaken the Dynamo defense— finding their stride, their rhythm, slipping into sync, and then as if hitting an overdrive gear, entered *the flow*—the unit suddenly breaking loose—flying into the Dynamo end in perfectly choreographed crisscrossing assaults, unleashing flash-firing rounds of peppering snap-shots, wrist-shots, rocket shots—and then finally scoring—and then scoring again—and then scoring again and again and again.

By game's end, Trotsky had scored once, Mikilov had scored twice, and the new player, the one who wore the number *seven*—Yuri Kershy—had scored four times to crush the Latvian Dynamos 8-2. And as the Red Army stepped off the ice that night to leave the Palace, the people of Moscow rose once again, in a *loud, thunderous red, banner-waving ovation.*

Next to fall were the legendary Soviet Wings, followed by Spartak, the Automobilists of Svordlodsk, the powerful Locomotive team, and then the power of Siberia: the mighty Traktor of Chelyabinsk—all falling hard and decisively, unable to stop the lightening, precision attacks⁻ of the Central Red Army's new front line of Trotsky, Mikilov, and Kershy.

And as the opponents fell, the stir brewed larger—in Moscow, as well as in the other National League cities—as people began to talk of this new young player—the one who wore the number *seven*. Those who had seen him in person, discussed the experience passionately, analyzing and describing his play as something different from anything they had ever seen—some comparing him to the American player of a few years prior, the late Tommy Haasen, *The American Magician.*

The interest rapidly expanded—spreading further and wider— and soon a craze began to ascend. Tickets for the Red Army games began to rise in demand as the curiosity of the populace grew. The demand soon escalated beyond what it had been when Kharlamov or Tretyak were playing, beyond what it had been when Trotsky had started playing. People began to flock to the games in massive numbers—unmanageable numbers— hording around the ticket boxes along Leningrad Boulevard, and around the Palace, all hoping for an opportunity to see the new player, the number *seven*— hoping to see him play, or move, or at least catch a passing glimpse.

Demand for the Red Army tickets skyrocketed further

and then went out of control, giving epidemic rise to *viyatka* and *defitstny* and soon extra police and KGB had to be put on in order to keep control around the long lines, and amongst the crowds. Black market tickets became nearly unpurchaseable, selling for outrageously large sums of money, some demanding American dollars rather than rubles—and the general public began to protest, demanding an end to the corruption, and demanding more coverage of the Red Army games on their radios and television sets.

Over the course of this season, Yuri grew his hair longer, just like Mikilov's—except his wasn't as blond—his was more sandy, sticking out of his helmet in a pixie, boyish sort of way. He soon became the new focus of youth and teenage attention, not only in Moscow, but across the entire nation. His picture began to appear on posters and calendars, and in magazines—photos of him in his illustrious red, blue, and gold Red Army uniform, the golden hammers and sickles embedded in the big blue stars on his shoulders, his twinkling green eyes smiling at the camera. The colorful posters and calendars flooded the country, going up on walls and over beds all across the nation—over the beds of young boys who had found a new hero, and the beds of teenage girls who suffered terrible crushes over him. He was interviewed in the newspapers and on television, and when the Soviet public saw and heard the young player with the twinkling eyes speak—speak so warmly and sincerely of his coaches and teammates and of his hometown friends and family in Letegorsk—he won the hearts of millions all across the land, young and old alike—becoming an even bigger sensation, not only in Russia and in the

Baltics, but amongst the non-hockey Republics to the south as well.

Later that season, the Red Army traveled to Sweden on a highly publicized trip, in which the Reds defeated the Swedish powerhouse by a score of 4-1, with Yuri Kershy scoring three of the Red Army's four goals. The city of Stockholm was vibrant with excitement—the arena filled with teenage girls inside and out, all who had come with the hopes of seeing the new teen idol from the U.S.S.R.

The following morning, a press session was scheduled at the Globe Hotel, in the main ballroom, and although it was the superstar Yuri Kershy they all wanted to see, Coach Sokolov demanded that the complete first line of Trotsky, Mikilov and Kershy answer the questions and do the autograph signing. Coach Sokolov had always upheld a strict policy that rarely allowed his players to be interviewed by foreigners, or to do foreign press conferences—especially with the Western press. Select interviews suggested that there were individual members of the team more worthy of note, or more significant than others, and in theory, this was never the case. But this new phenomenon, which had begun over the course of the season—and was now expanding beyond control—was something Sokolov had never encountered—at least not on the Red Army team, and certainly not to this magnitude. He had seen it on Western teams—the Swedes and the Americans a few years ago—and he had assumed it would remain in the West as a part of their culture, like the worship of rock and roll stars. But now it had become a part of his own club; it had entered his own household, and he knew he had to respond. Being a man of experimentation and progression, he decided that the best practice was to alter his policy, and under controlled conditions, allow the press session.

But when Coach Alexi Sokolov entered the hotel ballroom that following morning with his starting three players, he was completely taken aback—they were all taken aback. *Shocked.* There were girls everywhere—*shrieking girls*—gathered in groups of hundreds, maybe even thousands, mobbed in the parking lot and in the lobby and jammed into the ballroom. The Swedish police stood in chained lines trying to keep the stirring females a safe distance from the players, trying to protect them as they entered—pushing through the confusion of voices and flashing cameras, until they finally took their seats at the table behind the several bouquets of arranged microphones. The questions began almost immediately, most all of which were directed at Kershy; but to Coach Sokolov's admiration, the young player turned many of the questions over to his line mates, Trotsky and Mikilov, stating that they had the experience and wisdom to answer these things better than himself, and that he was still learning from them.

Although the weekend in Sweden proved to be successful, it had only been a test of Coach Sokolov's. When it came time for the Central Red Army to embark on their tour of Western Europe and then later to North America, Sokolov took Yuri aside and told him that he would not be making the trip—telling him that in a couple years he could maybe tour, but for now he was still young, and that he did not want him exposed to the violent game of the NHL, and that it would be best if he remained behind and concentrated on his studies at the University of Moscow. Yuri listened closely to Coach Sokolov's words and nodded obediently. Sokolov had readied himself for the boy's disappointment, but there seemed to be none, and from this, Sokolov could only conclude that Yuri was apparently still so thrilled to be a part of the team that disappointment in not being able to tour right away had not even entered his mind.

And so as the Central Red Army departed on their tour that year of Western Europe and North America, young Yuri Kershy remained behind, concentrating on his courses at the University of Moscow and training at the Red Army Sports School, continuing to live in near oblivion to the fact that he was not only the biggest celebrity on the University campus and in the city of Moscow, but in the entire nation. He continued to be the major topic of conversation in the markets and shops, and on the streets—where people passionately discussed his unique style of play, admiring and analyzing and arguing its finer points, but all beginning to agree that he was not only the best player in the world, but was most possibly the finest to ever live.

And there were other people—a rare few in actuality—around Moscow and in other cities and towns—not even necessarily hockey fans—who claimed that there was something else about the boy—something special, something *extraordinary.* They described it as a kind of *oddness* that surrounded him, a form of *light* that seemed to encase him and protect him and render him nearly untouchable—claiming that they could actually see it, that they could *actually physically see it.* "It's like a faint glow," they would say, trying to explain it to people who usually looked at them blankly, apparently not understanding... "It's like a strange sort of white light."

LAST STOP AT THE STOP 'N GO

September 1986

Just the two of them were in the store—the man and the checkout girl. The man was older, his hair graying—probably approaching fifty. He wore baggy jeans with cheap designer stitching, an old nylon quilted coat and a new camouflage hunting cap tipped ahead and a little to one side. In his arms he cradled the items he had gathered from the shelves: a couple boxes of pink and white Good 'n Plentys, three boxes of Gummi Bears, a one-pound bag of *fun-size* Snickers bars, a bag of Reese's Pieces, some Red Licorice, four boxes of Chiclets, and a box of cherry-flavored cough drops—all heaped in a colorful pile atop a small stack of magazines which he supported with his hands from beneath.

The checkout girl had watched the man pick everything out from her place behind the counter. She was considerably younger than him, and although once chubby in figure, was now frail, even gaunt in stature. Her heartbeat was beginning to increase as she considered what it was that she was about to do. Her life had been lived demurely—never asserting herself, never raising her hand or her voice—and now her time was running out, her days were slipping away. She readjusted her oversized smock and touched her hand to her hair as the man approached, then she started into the pile as he set it down in front of her—sorting through the items with one hand while pushing buttons with the other. It was time to take a chance.

"How much for the sweet rolls?" asked the man. He reached for the clear plastic cover along the counter and lifted it.

"Um, let's see," said the girl; she nudged her glasses back onto her cheeks—fat-rimmed owl glasses with slumped bows. "The bismarcks are sixty-five, and the jelly rolls are fifty."

"I better have a jelly," said the man, and he pulled out a big white-frosted one with purple oozing out the side. The girl added the fifty into the register and continued with the pile. Under the Good 'n Plentys and Gummi Bears was the first of the magazines slowly becoming exposed. A promiscuously positioned cover girl lay there in skimpily fringed lingerie: a copy of *Hustler.*

"Been grouse huntin'?" asked the girl. Her heartbeat accelerated further.

"Oh, some," said the man. "Too much cover yet though, a guy can't hardly see nothin'."

"Yeah, we need a good frost," said the girl anxiously. "It might help straighten this weather out some too."

"Oh, I been gettin' a few here 'n 'nare, I 'spose," said the man. "But hell, it ain't really no use yet, ya know."

The girl nudged up on her glasses again. "Oh, I bet you're just being modest now. You're gettin' all kinds of birds I'll bet."

"I better have me a couple of them too," said the man. He had spotted a jar of beef jerky on the counter — just next to the sweet rolls. He untwisted the lid and dug down inside.

"You been huntin' mostly alone then, er?"

"How much are these?" asked the man.

"The jerkys? Thirty-five each," said the girl.

"I better grab me another one too," said the man, and he reached in again. The girl added the jerkys to the tally, then took hold of another magazine poking its price into the register. A copy of *High Society*. The cover girl lay sprawled back in a filmy gauze of satin and lace, her arms stretched above her head clutching large bedposts.

"So what else ya been up to?" asked the girl nervously. "Been keepin' yourself outta trouble?"

"Oh, I don't know, I 'spose," said the man. He lifted his hat by the bill, scratching his head some, then set it back on with a slight adjustment, tipping it further to the side and a bit more forward. His eyes squinted at a pyramid stack of shotgun shells on the counter — just beyond the jerky jar. A red tag discount special. *Four-ninety-eight*. "Better throw a box of them on there too," he said, then reached over and picked off a box and plopped it down on top of the magazines. *Super-Shot* express loads. Three inch magnum, number eight shot. Underneath lay a copy of *Swank*—the cover girl perched atop red satin sheets in scanty black lingerie, her hair blown back, her lips parted, her eyes looking foggily at the viewer.

"It's a good price on them shells," said the girl taking hold of the box, her thin fingers stabbing buttons.

"Yeah, hell, they kill 'em as good as anything, far as I can tell," said the man.

"It's all my brothers ever use,' said the girl. "They say there's no sense in buying Federals or Winchesters or nothin' like that when you can get *these*—and they *seem* just as good."

The man reached into his drooped rear pocket and dug out his wallet. He pulled out a ten and some crumpled singles. The girl pushed the *total* button and then awkwardly yanked out a bag. She began placing the items in, then paused to run her hand along her hair again. She looked at the man as she flicked it, trying to toss it back, but it didn't go anywhere, it had become too thin now and weightless.

"Don't it get kind of boring huntin' alone all the time?" asked the girl. Her heartbeat began to accelerate again.

"Huh?" said the man. He was turned completely around, focused on something else.

"I mean, you ever think of goin' with someone else, or takin' somebody along or somethin'?"

The man mumbled something, almost inaudibly. He was staring across at the video selection, his eyes absorbing them one at a time— *First Blood—Kill Or Be Killed— Deadly Silence*—then skipping down past three shelves of dramas and family pictures to—*Cheerleader Weekend—Naughty Prom Queen—*

"You seen the movie yet?" asked the girl, her voice suddenly rising to a higher, livelier level.

The man turned back to the counter. "Huh?"

"You seen the movie? At the Royal?"

"No," said the man. "What's playin'?"

"Oh, I don't know," said the girl shrugging her skeletal shoulders. "I just thought maybe *you* might know."

"Nuh, I couldn't tell ya," said the man.

"I don't know what it is either," said the girl, "but I think it's 'sposed to be somethin' good." She swallowed and took a weak breath. "Would you like to go or somethin', sometime, Don?"

The man's forehead crinkled into a confused frown. "How much damage ya got there?"

"Um... twenty-eighty-six," said the girl. Her heart pounded as her magnified eyes watched the man's hand peel through the money... then they snuck up and watched his lips mouthing numbers, his eyes busy counting...

"There's twenty-one," said the man.

The girl turned to the till and rang it open, then dipped her trembling fingers down into the trays, sliding out the coins. She nudged her heavy glasses back onto her cheeks again. "Fourteen cents is your change," she said. "Want the magazines in the bag?"

"Yeah, I 'spose," said the man.

The girl's fragile hand gripped the gloss-covered beauties and slid them down inside with the candy and shells; then she held the bag up for the man. "There you go," she said, and gave him another smile.

"Okee-dokee," said the man. He took the bag and turned for the door.

The girl reached up and ran her hand along her hair again. "Thank you now," she said.

"You bet," the man answered back.

The girl's eyes followed the man, watching him lean his weight against the door, pushing out, his arm clutching close the bag of new possessions. "Hurry back now!" she called after him.

"You bet," his voice answered back.

The girl's eyes blinked—blinked anxiously behind her thick lenses. She took a big breath and suddenly blurted after the man in a voice she had never before known, *"Don't be a stranger now!"*

But there was nothing in return. The new found voice had received no response... only the sound of the door swinging slowly closed between them.

STRANGER'S DAY

Summer 1976

Space entered Jorgenson's Food and Mercantile, moving straight to the back of the store. He wore faded jeans and dingo boots and a skin tight t-shirt with a pack of Marlboro's rolled up in the shoulder. At eighteen he was small for his age, but he walked fast and bold with his chest forward in a very *Billy the Kid* sort of manner.

Like most of the stores along Main Street, Jorgenson's was an old turn of the century building with creaky boarded floors and a high tin-type ceiling. The store sold most of the groceries in Borg, plus various other goods of local necessity, such as rakes and pails—rubber boots and Big Mac coveralls—all packed in high and tightly into six narrow aisles.

Space stopped at the rear corner of the store, at the shelf with the Hallmark greeting cards. The cards were divided into small-labeled bins according to holiday or occasion. Space scanned the rack, finding the Father's Day section, then touched gently over the remaining cards. There were four. Father's Day had long passed, it was now July. He looked at the cards closely, holding each of them individually. The one he finally chose was the most serious, most expensive looking of the four. It was done in soft flower-gauzed colors with glossy golden print across the front that said: *"To My Father on This Special Day."*

Space pulled the matching envelope from the bin and headed for the till.

The Jorgenson girl looked down at the card on the counter, then up at Space. He was hoping she would make a remark about it—a wise-crack or something—because he was ready for her if she did.

But the Jorgenson girl said nothing. She just turned her blue eyes to the till and rang it up. Probably because she knew it was *real,* Space figured. That's right, she probably knew that it wasn't BS anymore. She knew now that *it was for real.*

Space took his change and headed for the door, then glanced back at the Jorgenson girl before going out, giving her a final *Told ya so!* grin. Then he stepped out the door into the afternoon sun.

His Plymouth Barracuda was the only vehicle in front of the store—a jacked up 71 model with wheels, the works, all decked out with shag carpet on the inside, and a '76 graduation tassel that dangled from the rearview mirror. The remainder of Main Street was dead; just a handful of pickups sat nosed into the curb down by the cafe. The day was hot and still; the only sounds—the only life—seemed to be the afternoon crickets and cicadas buzzing in the humidity.

Space stopped alongside his Barracuda and opened the card, then laid it on top of his shiny purple hood. He pulled out a pen and then signed carefully at the bottom: *Love Tim.*

He closed the card and sealed it in the envelope, then wrote carefully on the front of it... *"Dad."* Then he turned for his driver's door—about to open it—when he heard an approaching engine. He glanced back to see a red Chevy SS coming down the street—a '69 model—*Swanson and Ullendahl—runningback and quarterback—*Ullendahl leaning on his elbow out the passenger side, a big grin on his face as they pulled up out front.

"Hey, Spaceman! This the big day?"

"That's right, Ullendork!" said Space. "And I don't wanna see you women anywhere near that place, ya hear?"

"Yeah, yeah, yeah," said Ullendahl. He said it like he'd been told a hundred times already. He leaned back into the car and said something to Swanson, and Swanson broke out in laughter. Then Ullendahl looked at Space again. "Ya nervous?"

"Nervous?" said Space. *"About what?"*

"Well, you know," said Ullendahl. "I mean, are you ready for all this wealth and this big time life you're gonna start living?"

Space opened the door of his Barracuda and took a pair of sunglasses off the dash. "I've had my whole life to get ready for it, I sure as hell should be."

Swanson said something to Ullendahl again, inside the car, and they both broke out laughing. Space put his sunglasses on and held his stare on the two. His sunglasses were mirrors, just like the over-the-road truckers wore that hauled grain over to Duluth.

"See you bozos in the funnies," he said. Then he got into his Barracuda and fired up the big 426 hemi. He backed the *rumbling* machine away from the curb and then stepped on the accelerator—*squealing* out—laying a patch in front of the Chevy SS, and a streak of rubber all the way down the block, halfway to the cafe.

Swanson and Ullendahl remained behind in the empty street, their motor idling, watching the purple Barracuda squeal off around the corner that led out to Highway 75.

"Is he nuts, or what?"

"I don't know," said Ullendahl.

"I mean, you think this bullshit is real?"

2

The Barracuda rocketed out of town past the town sign, and then another sign that stood against the trees alongside—a large homemade billboard that read from the other side:

Welcome to Borg
516 people live here
If you're one of them
you're home now

Space slapped in the eight track, blasting the car full of rock and roll—Nazareth's *Hair Of The Dog*. His boot double-stepped the clutch as he shifted into fourth—shifting just like the grain haulers did—powering the shiny purple hood scoop out over the hot bleached concrete of Highway 75. As he barreled the machine north across the wide open fields of amber and green, he bobbed and sang passionately with the eight track— "Now you're messin' with a... son of a— now you're messin' with a son-of-a-bitch!"

3

Four miles northeast of Borg, an old Ford pickup with Cat mud flaps pulled in across the vacant parking lot of Pepper-Dines Tap & Grill. The vehicle stopped outside the front windows—in front of the one with the *closed* sign in it. Two farm boys stepped out—a big, stocky kid with a Cenex cap, and another—the driver—a strong, lean kid with cowboy boots and a light mesh muscle shirt.

Pepper-Dines was a small roadside place with a scrub-weed parking lot and a faded neon sign out by the highway. An old whitewash farmhouse and a couple red barns stood a short distance behind. The two farm boys glanced around at the empty gravel lot, then headed for the propped-open front doorway and strolled inside.

"How do?" said the lean one.

Jenny looked up from behind the counter where she was just setting a pan of chicken into the oven. She was eighteen, same as the others— dressed in a clean white blouse with short sleeves. She was slightly plump in figure with soft, friendly eyes. "How you guys?" she said.

"Good, good."

"We ain't open, you know."

"Yeah, we just stopped by to say hi to the Spacer."

"He ain't showed up yet," said Jenny. "Should be here

any minute, though."

The stocky one grinned. "So that rich old man of his is finally comin', uh?"

Jenny looked at the stocky one. "Uh huh," she said, and turned away from him.

"Comin' in a big limo I 'spose," said the stocky one. "Loaded with diamonds and cash and the whole works I'll bet, huh?" He slapped his hand down on the counter and let out a short fabricated laugh.

Jenny ignored it, keeping her back to the two.

The lean one stepped towards the windows and looked out. "I don't think she finds it very funny."

"No, I don't," said Jenny.

The stocky one looked at the lean one, then at Jenny again. His big smirk began to settle... *"What,"* he said. "What, are you guys startin' to believe this crap?"

4

The purple Barracuda swung back onto highway 75 and accelerated north for a mile, then veered off onto County Road 17, forking into the northeast, heading for Pepper-Dines. Space throttled the big 426 hemi, fully decked now in new slacks and shoes, and a brand new polyester shirt. The shirt was bright peach with yellow swirls and blue flowers, almost looking Hawaiian. He wore it unbuttoned at the chest, a gold chain around his neck, his sleeves rolled neatly to the elbows. His hair was puffed and blow combed—bobbing to Peter Frampton on the eight track—his shades reflecting sun as he checked himself in the rearview.

A mile up 17, Space downshifted again—bouncing the Barracuda in rumbling jerks—then pulled into Pepper-Dines lot charging the accelerator again, fish-tailing across the gravel. He hit the brakes and skidded to a dusty stop alongside the old Ford pickup, then jumped out and headed in through the opened front doorway.

"You guys lost or somethin'?"

"Whoa!" cried the stocky kid—his face had lit with a big grin again. "Holy shit, man, check out the duds!"

"This place is closed, boys!'

"Where'd ya get them, Spaceman, off a dead faggot?"

Space answered back but it was lost in an outburst of hysterical laughter, especially from the stocky one. He was a tackle on the football team—*Haugen.* The lean one, *Smitty,* was a receiver—Ullendahl's main man.

"What's with the hairdo Spacecase? What are you 'sposed to be, a poodle or a fag or what?"

There was more laughter, and Space responded louder, shouting through it, *"Get the hell out of here!"*

"Ah c'mon, Spaceman" said Smitty. "We just stopped by to check it out."

"Well, ya got it checked out," said Space, "so now *check out!"*

Haugen looked at Space again with his big puffy smirk. "So it's no shit now Spacecase, he's really comin', huh?"

"That's right, Haugen-Schmaugen!" said Space. He went up to Haugen, right up to his big barrel chest. "Why, you still think I'm bullshittin'? Huh?"

Haugen's grin faded a notch.

Space turned to Smitty. "How 'bout you, Smitty? You still think I'm full of shit? Huh? Do ya?"

Smitty didn't answer; he just folded his arms and ran his

eyes over the new clothes again.

Space's mirrors shifted between the two of them. "You clowns ain't got much to say about it now, do ya? Huh?"

It was quiet for a moment except for the overhead whirling of a fan. Then Smitty turned for the door. "Well, everybody'll be over at the Hi-Ho tonight, Spaceman, in case you wanna stop by and introduce us all."

"If you're lucky!" said Space. He said it in a cocky snap.

Haugen followed after Smitty, giving Space another grin with raised eyebrows as he went out the door. "Sure like them threads."

"Yeah, and I like that ugly face you got, Haugen!" said Space. He followed them to the doorway and watched them return to their pickup; then he turned back to Jenny. "How do I look?" he said. "Okay?"

Jenny smiled from behind the counter. "Yeah," she said, "you look good."

"No, tell me, really, how do I look?"

5

Outside, the doors slammed closed on the Ford pickup. Then Haugen said, "Well, whata'ya think?"

Smitty didn't answer. He took his sunglasses off the dash and pushed in the clutch.

"I mean, you think this guy's really comin'?"

Smitty slid his sunglasses on, then lowered his hand to the ignition and started the engine. "There's no such thing as *this guy,*" he said. Then he shifted into reverse and backed them out across the gravel.

6

Space moved to the front windows with a bottle of Schmidt beer, his mirrors watching the Ford pickup pull back onto the county highway. Then he turned to Jenny again. "C'mon now, tell me the truth, do I look goofy or what?"

"You look nice, Tim, you really do."

Space grinned and looked back out the windows, craning his view to the north, settling his eyes on the far horizon, where the amber and green met the blue. Canada. He took a swallow of Schmidt, then said, "Been a long time... I don't know what this is gonna be like, man, *fifteen years*. I don't even know what he looks like." Then he let out an anxious breath. "Like a tycoon, I 'spose."

A fly buzzed somewhere in the windows—between the glass and one of the red checkered curtains...

"I need some tunes!"

Space turned and started across the floor, crossing to the jukebox along the far wall. He dropped a quarter in and started pushing buttons. Then he arched himself back and said, "I'm gettin' out've here, man! Finally gettin outta this lousy town!" He looked across at Jenny. "You are too, remember! Soon as I get up there and check it out, I'm lettin' you know and then you're comin' up too!"

Jenny gave him a smile, and Fleetwood Mac started to strum *Rhiannon*. Space started to bob his head and tap his new shoe... then he started into a one man dance.

7

A lone car coming from the north pulled to a dusty stop along the gravel shoulder of county road 17, several hundred feet north of Pepper-Dines. A man stepped out on the passenger's side, and then the car pulled out and accelerated away.

The man stood on the narrow shoulder looking towards the small roadside club up ahead. He stared at it for several minutes, long after the car he'd stepped from had disappeared, leaving only the prairie wind blowing across. The man was lean, chiseled and expressionless, wearing baggy flapping pants and a loose cotton shirt. He was around forty, but had a weathered, worn exterior that made him seem older. He slid his calloused hands into his pockets and started down the gravel shoulder.

8

As the music selection faded to an end in Pepper-Dines, Space began pacing about, speaking in multiple mimicking voices: "'You're so full of shit, Space!' 'Oh sure Space, *sure!*' '*Oh,* yeah, I'll bet, I'll bet!' 'You lyin' sacka' shit, Spacecase!'"

He stopped and looked at Jenny again. "I'm gonna show them suckers, man! They'll see I wasn't such a bullshitter after all! Bunch of farm brains. That's all they are, Jenny, all these people around here. Bunch've goddamn farm brains! They don't know shit!"

Space started towards the counter and sat down on a stool, then glanced across towards the windows. "They'll

all be sittin' over at the Hi-Ho tonight thinkin' 'bout me."
He started to take a drink but then hesitated. "You know
what we should do? We should go over there later and
show them boneheads."

Jenny started to say something but it went
unheard—

"Wonder what he drives? Cadillac or Mercedes or
somethin', I'll bet. Yeah, that's what we'll do, eh—we'll
go down there in his Cadillac and we'll show them stupid
bastards!"

"This has nothing to do with the others, Tim."

Space looked at Jenny.

"Don't worry about them, Tim. Really."

"Shit, I forgot I had a card for him!"

Space jumped off his stool and started quickly for the
door, then stopped to look back at Jenny before going out.
"Sure I look okay?"

Jenny smiled again. "Yeah, I'm sure."

Space turned again, to rush out the doorway, but as he
did, bumped into the man off the highway. "Whoa! Sorry
there, bud."

The man off the highway remained in the open
doorway as Space hustled past, then he looked in at Jenny.
"Boy's in a hurry," he said. His voice was coarse and
weathered like his skin.

Jenny smiled. "People around here call him 'Space'".

"Space," the man said to himself.

"Yeah, 'cause they say that's where his head's at most
the time. Can I get you somethin'?"

The man started in towards the counter. "Uh..."

"Wanna beer, or a drink or somethin'?"

"Uh, no, um... a Coke, I 'spose, would be fine."

Jenny pulled out a glass and reached for the fountain dispenser; then said cheerfully, "Where you from? Not from around here, are you?"

"No," said the man. "No, I'm, uh... just a stranger."

Jenny set the glass of Coke in front of the man and smiled again.

"Well, that'll be forty cents, stranger."

9

Space took the card from the front seat of the Barracuda then shut the door and walked out across the scrub-weed gravel towards the highway. A lone car was approaching from the north, coming fast. Space stopped and waited, his mirrors reflecting sun as he watched the vehicle draw near...

The car whistled past.

Space looked both ways again... Nothing...

10

"Smells good in here," said the stranger. He had sat down on a stool at the near end of the counter—at the L— his back to the door.

Jenny nodded towards the oven. "Chicken."

"You make it?"

"Yeah, it's for him and his dad." Jenny tipped her head towards the windows. "They're having sort of a reunion here today. They haven't seen each other in awhile."

The stranger nodded. "Sounds nice."

"In fact, really we're closed today. My folks aren't even

openin'—it's kinda so they'd have a nice place for it."

"Should be here any minute," said Space. He breezed back in through the open doorway, then went to the front windows and looked out at the highway again, craning his view into the north.

"That's nice of you to get a card for him," said Jenny.

"Ah, it's kinda sappy, but I'm sure he's sorta sentimental about all this, so I got it for him. He kinda goes for the sentimental stuff, ya know."

"Well, it was thoughtful of you."

Space glanced at the stranger. "How you doin', bud?"

The stranger answered without looking at Space. "Fine, thank you."

"This place is closed, ya know."

"He knows," said Jenny.

Space looked back out the windows, then sat down on the edge of a table, on the red checkered cloth, setting his feet up on a chair.

The stranger said, "Big day for you, I hear."

"Huh?" said Space. "Oh, yeah—yeah, I guess everybody kinda knows about it." He glanced towards the clock over the counter, "What time is it?"

"Almost quarter after," said Jenny.

"He oughta be here any time now."

"Where's he coming from?" asked the stranger.

"Winnipeg," said Space.

The stranger nodded to himself. "Long way."

Space craned himself along the windows again and looked up the highway, as far into the north as he could see. "Ever been to Canada, bud?"

The stranger didn't respond for a moment. Then he said, "Yeah."

Jenny glanced at the stranger, meeting his eyes, then looked away.

"How ya like it?" asked Space.

The stranger hesitated again, then said, "It's different."

"I hear it's nice, though," said Space. "I might be goin' up there. To live with my dad."

"Is that right."

"Yeah, that's right."

The stranger took a swallow of his Coke, then said, "What's he do?"

"He's an executive. Of a big corporation up there."

Jenny's eyes shifted to the stranger again. He was looking ahead at nothing in particular.

"Does well for himself, eh?" said the stranger.

"'Well' ain't the word for it," said Space proudly.

The stranger finished his Coke and set the empty glass ahead on the counter.

Jenny glanced at Space, then back at the stranger. "You, um, you want another one?"

Space turned around. The stranger nodded to Jenny.

"Hey, uh, Jenny, he's gonna be here any minute, ya know."

The stranger said to Jenny, "Am I interfering with—"

"No," said Jenny, "that's fine."

"I thought this place was closed to the public today," said Space.

"He's just havin' a Coke, Tim."

Space looked at the stranger again. "You gonna be here long, or you got somewhere to go or somethin', er?"

Tim," said Jenny firmly.

"I won't be long," said the stranger. "I'm to meet someone shortly, so I won't be long."

Space held his mirrors on the stranger's profile... then he turned back to the windows. Jenny's eyes met the stranger's again, but this time did not look away. The stranger's eyes shifted to the clock over the counter, which read 3:15.

11

At four o'clock, the stranger was still at the counter, and Space was still at the window, smoking a cigarette. The Father's Day card lay on the table alongside, next to the mirror sunglasses and a couple empty bottles of Schmidt.

Jenny went to the oven and poked at the chicken. "We gotta eat this soon if were gonna eat it warm."

"He'll be here any second," said Space. "Just hold on."

"Well, I can save some for him." Jenny looked at the stranger. "You hungry?"

Space spun around. "Hey, what are ya doin'?"

"What."

"I thought that was for *us.*"

"Well, it is," said Jenny, "but there's plenty."

"That ain't the point."

"It's been in the oven too long, Tim."

"Ah, don't you gotta be somewhere or somethin', bud?"

"*Hey!*" said Jenny. Her eyes were set firmly on Space again. "I got all this chicken and no one to eat it! Now, I said there's plenty, okay?"

Space blinked, then looked at the stranger's profile again. He tamped out his cigarette, then turned back to the windows.

12

At 4:35, a couple plates of chicken bones sat discarded on the counter. Space sat on a stool, just off the corner of the L, drinking another Schmidt. He watched the stranger eating off a drumstick, staring at him for long periods of time, his eyes beginning to dim with some early signs of drunkenness. Jenny kept herself back, standing at the far end of the counter.

"What's that?" said Space.

The stranger kept his eyes downward, his attention towards his plate. "What," he said.

Space pointed at the stranger's forearm. "Right there."

The stranger took another bite. "Tattoo."

"I can see *that,*" said Space. "What is it?"

"Nothing," said the stranger. "Means nothing."

Space leaned in closer. "What's that say?. . Bull"—

The stranger covered it with his sleeve.

"Bull - Riv... er," said Space, slowly. Then he said, "*Bull River?*" He sat upright on his stool. "The prison?... North Dakota?"

The stranger took another bite off his drumstick...

"You were in prison?" said Space. "Holy sh— Hey Jenny, this guy you gave our chicken to is a goddamn ex-con!" Space looked at the stranger again. "Holy shit, man, what did ya do?"

"Tim—"

"Just a minute," said Space. He put a hand up towards Jenny keeping his eyes on the stranger. "What did ya do, man? I mean, what were ya in for?"

The stranger looked into the side of his Coke glass as he

chewed. "It doesn't matter."

"Oh, come on, tell me," said Space. He slid in a bit closer. "What did ya do?"

"Tim—"

"Robbery? Arson?"

"Tim, he told you it wasn't important, okay?"

"Murder?"

The stranger lowered the drumstick and looked at Space, looking directly at him for the first time. He looked into his eyes, with his natural deadpan of tired, unwavering eyes.

Space blinked and sat up on his stool again. "Ah, yeah," he said. He swallowed deeply and forced a quick smile, "Yeah, what the hell, it don't really matter, does it?"

The stranger held his eyes on Space, and Space swallowed again, then turned and stumbled off his stool. He moved away, walking to the far end of the counter, to where Jenny was standing.

"Get this guy outta here." He said it in a hushed whisper.

"Why?" said Jenny quietly. "What's he doin'?"

"Nothin'," said Space. "There's just somethin' about him."

"Tim, I can't jus—"

"Get him out!"

"Well, let him at least finish eati—"

"I won't be long," came the voice from the other end of the counter.

Space spun around, meeting the stranger's stare again.

The stranger slid his finished plate of chicken bones ahead of him, then lit a cigarette, not taking his eyes off Space. Jenny moved quietly down the counter and took the plate. Space looked down and away, avoiding the stranger's stare. He rubbed the side of his head, then readjusted his shirt...

"I shot a man."

"Huh?" said Space. His head jerked upward, looking at the stranger again—his heart starting to pound. "Oh, that—oh hey, ah—you don't have to tell me—"

"No, you asked, didn't you?"

"Well, yeah, but—"

"So now you know," said the stranger. He took a slow drag off his cigarette. "I killed a person."

Space swallowed deeply again, feeling a slow bead of sweat start down his back. He could feel the stranger's stare, but avoided it, glancing about the floor and at the walls... He finally took a deep breath and forced another smile. "Well, uh... what did you uh, what did you do that for?"

"What."

"Ah, shoo—" Space cleared his throat and rubbed at his chin. "Ah, what did ya shoot the guy for—I mean, you don't have to tell me—"

"Because he was going to shoot me."

Space looked at the stranger... then released a breath, and smiled. "Well, heck, that's self-defense then, ain't it?"

"I was robbing his store."

"Oh," said Space. He nodded to himself and his smile disappeared. He looked down at his new shoes... then said, "What kinda store?"

"Grocery store."

Space looked up again. "Big one?"

"No."

Space nodded to himself. "Oh," he said, then looked at Jenny, meeting her eyes for a moment, then looked off towards the wall. "Well, uh... what were you robbin' a grocery store for?"

"I was hungry."

Space looked at the stranger again, then broke out laughing...

The stranger took another slow drag off his cigarette and exhaled the smoke. Then he said, "So was my wife and kid."

The laughter stopped. Space glanced at Jenny again, and she looked away. Then she started for the door.

"Where you goin'?"

"Outside."

"What?"

"Just to get some air."

Space started after her. "Well wait, where ya goin'?"

Jenny looked back at him as she went out the open doorway, "Just out here."

Space followed after Jenny, stopping her just outside. "Wait!" he said, his tone hushed again. "Don't go leavin' me alone in there with that guy."

"I'll be right here, Tim, it's not like I'm goin' to Europe or anything."

"Well wait a second, don't leave! I mean, what if my dad comes now? I don't wanna be sittin' alone in there talkin' to some lunatic wino—"

"Don't say that!" said Jenny, her voice hushed again. "You don't even know him! So don't say that!"

Space blinked again, several times and Jenny turned and walked on.

"I'll be out here."

Space watched her walk off across the gravel. He started to follow, but then stopped. Then he turned and went back inside.

The stranger hadn't moved.

Space walked over to the windows and looked out again, looking again at Jenny. Then he looked up the highway, into the north, staring at the horizon with all his strength. He focused on it with all the concentration he had, as if—if only he could will it strongly enough— he could force the appearance of that big shiny Cadillac with the Manitoba plates.

"Nice girl."

Space flinched, then looked over his shoulder at the stranger. Then he looked back out the window again. "Yeah."

"Girlfriend?"

"Yeah."

"How long?"

"Couple of years," said Space. He looked at Jenny again, out in the middle of the lot. She was standing in the sun in her bright white blouse, the breeze touching her hair, her hands holding a single weed, stroking it gently...

"You afraid of me?"

Space turned towards the stranger again and his heart started to accelerate. "Why should I be afraid of you?"

The stranger shrugged, exhaling a slow breath of smoke, then tamped his cigarette out in an ashtray on the counter.

"I ain't afraid of you," said Space.

"Maybe you just don't like who I am."

"I don't give a shit who you are," said Space. Then he caught the stare again, the stranger's eyes looking directly at him. He turned from it, and looked back out the windows. "Hey look, I don't care, okay? All I want is for my dad to show up, that's all. I don't know where he is, but—"

Space stopped himself and hesitated for a moment... Then he turned and picked up the card off the table and rushed out the open doorway.

Jenny looked up from the middle of the lot, seeing Space striding fast towards his car. She called out to him, "Where ya goin'?"

"The Hi-Ho!"

Jenny started towards him. "Well wait, what for?"

"I bet he got mixed up and went over there!"

"Well wait, just a minute—what'a'ya mean?"

"That's gotta be what happened," said Space. He opened the door of his Barracuda and got in. "I'm sure that's where he is!"

"Well, wait Tim—why don't you just call over there? *Hey!*"

Space started his engine and began backing away— then he shouted out his window, "I'll be right back! And get this guy outta here, will ya?"

The Barracuda spun around, churning up gravel and dust then charged off across the lot and onto highway 17.

Jenny stood watching the car accelerate away, moving quickly off to the south. She watched the shiny purple fade smaller and quieter, until it finally disappeared into the distant green and blue.

13

Jenny went back inside, walking slowly past the stranger—who hadn't moved... She stopped part-way down the counter and leaned back against it.

More flies buzzed in the windows... A cyclone of dust meandered across the lot outside...

The stranger lit another cigarette...

Jenny looked down at her tennis shoes, then finally said, "So where you from?" Her hands gripped the counter firmly behind herself...

The stranger told Jenny that he'd previously been from North Dakota, but said he'd left his place of residence there one night under *Not very acceptable circumstances.* He told her that, *by law,* he wasn't welcome in North Dakota any longer—or Minnesota for that matter—or *anywhere* in the U.S.

Jenny said nothing.

The stranger asked about her boyfriend.

Jenny looked at the stranger, then looked down at her shoes again. She told the stranger that Tim's mother had sold their house and moved out west with a friend a couple months back, and that Tim had found his dad's address— his address in *Canada*—cleaning the place out. She told of how Tim had moved to Borg with his mother when he was only three, telling how they had come from... *from North Dakota*—and how he was the only boy in Borg without a dad. She told of how Tim had always wanted to be like the other boys, but just wasn't—how he'd always tried to keep up with them and compete with them growing up. She told of how he had gone out for football and basketball when he'd gotten older—but explained that he wasn't as big as the other boys, so he didn't get to play very much. She told of how Tim had to sit on the bench and watch, as the other boys scored all the points for Borg—and won all the victories, and then got praised by their fathers after the games, and got their pictures in the *Tri-County Reporter*.

When Jenny looked at the stranger again, he was staring down at the counter top...

"And so his dad just kept gettin' bigger and more magnificent all the time, you see? It was like... I dunno... a *defense.* A defense or somethin', you know?" She looked towards the windows, looking out at the highway and the fields beyond. "And he lives it."

14

Space's Barracuda spun into the parking lot at the Hi-Ho and skidded to a stop. The Hi-Ho sat on the west edge of town, behind the tracks and the elevator. The parking lot was scattered with local vehicles—muscle cars, four-wheel drives—pickups with gun racks and mud flaps. Space stepped out of his purple Barracuda scanning the cars, then headed for the door.

Inside, it was crowded, noisy and smoky—the place alive with *voices* and *clacking* pool balls and Jay Fergusson singing *Thunder Island* from the jukebox. As Space entered, the clientele's attention shifted to him like a magnet, going straight to the flowery shirt—

"Hey Spaceman!" yelled out one of them— *"Whoa!"* howled another—"Hey Spacecase, what the hell, you turnin' queer on us now boy?" There was laughter and whistling—"Where's that rich old man of yours, Spaceface?"—"Hey I like your blouse man, that's pretty nice!"

Space snapped back at one of them. "Why don't you just shut your ugly face, Halverson!"

"Oo-oo-oo-oohhh!" said Halverson, mocking scared with big round eyes.

There was more laughter and jeering. Space struggled through the crowd, crossing through a broad shaft of sun and dust particles that glowed in through the west windows, working his way up to the bar. Another burst of laughter rose out of the back corner as a remark carried across, warning somebody to be careful not to bend over in front of him.

"How are ya Tim?" said the bartender. He was an older man with an expressionless face.

"There hasn't been a guy here lookin' for me, has there?" asked Space. "An older guy kinda?"

"This is all that's been in, right here," said the bartender.

Space turned and glanced around again, surrounded by the pack of heckling voices and gleaming eyes.

"Beer?" asked the bartender.

Space shook his head.

"Hey Spaceface, where the hell is he?"

Space's eyes shifted to the voice—an older farm boy with muscles and a beard. He was setting his cigarette along the edge of the pool table, lining up a shot, his red Massy cap glowing under the Schmidt light.

''He um…''

"C'mon," said the older farm boy, "how long you gonna keep us poor wretched souls waitin'? We all wanna meet this rich ol' man of yours."

Space cleared his throat. "Well, he, um, he's gonna be here pretty soon now."

"Yeah I 'spose," said the older farm boy. Then he *cracked* the balls hard, firing one into the corner pocket.

More remarks cackled across the bar followed by more haranguing and laughter. Space stood teetering in his new shoes like a wary-eyed deer, his eyes darting and shifting—cornered, surrounded...

At a table in the near corner, sat Smitty and Haugen, Swanson, Ullendahl, and the Jorgenson girl—all five of them motionless, watching as the others continued to ridicule and tease. The Jorgenson girl started to get up, but then stopped when Space suddenly turned and bolted for the door, chased by more heckling and laughter.

Space staggered out into the lot, moving quickly away from the place. He gulped for air as he wandered back across the gravel, the laughter rising and swelling behind him. His eyes scanned the vehicles again, looking at every one of them, then looking beyond, turning, looking in all directions...

15

"So what happens if this man doesn't show?"

Jenny looked at the stranger... then looked down again. "He's not going to." She stared at her tennis shoe, tapping it silently on the floor. "Tim has a good job... with my uncle, working on his farm. My uncle wants him to start hauling grain too, over the road, to Duluth... He'll be alright."

"You like him?"

Jenny looked towards the windows. "Yeah," she said. "Yeah, I do. He just has to get rid of this crutch he keeps leanin' on, that's all." She looked at the stranger again, then back down at her shoe. "But I can't do that for him."

The sound of an approaching car began to grow out of the distance—becoming more distinct—coming from the south. Then the purple Barracuda appeared through the windows, turning into the lot outside. It pulled to a slow stop up by the front door.

16

Space stepped out of the Barracuda and closed the door, the card in hand. He walked slowly around his car, then paced in a small circle. He stopped and looked at the open entryway of Pepper-Dines, then walked over and leaned against the front of the building, in the shade, looking out at the highway again—looking again into the north...

The shadows had grown long by the time the stranger stepped back out the front entryway of Pepper-Dines. He stopped just outside and turned to Jenny behind him.

"Thank you," he said.

Jenny nodded to the stranger, and then the stranger turned and started away, walking off across the lot.

Space glanced at the stranger, then looked beyond him, looking again towards the highway. "Takin' off?"

The stranger kept walking, not looking. "Yeah."

"See ya."

"Was nice to meet you," said the stranger.

"Yeah, me too," said Space.

The stranger was halfway across the lot when he finally stopped. He turned around and looked at Space. "I didn't get your name," he said.

Space didn't look at the stranger, just said, "Space."

The stranger nodded. "Nice to meet you."

"Yeah," said Space.

The stranger just kept looking at Space—standing out in the middle of the sun-bleached lot like a gunfighter, a gust of dust rolling past...

Space ignored the gaze, keeping his eyes focused beyond the stranger, on the highway, *concentrating* into the north with all of his strength...

When the stranger spoke again, it was in a different tone, a different voice than what he had spoken in before. It was in a gentle, personal tone. He said, "Goodbye Tim."

Space's eyes shot back to the stranger. His heart jumped up into his throat and was suddenly pumping aggressively—pulling the strength from his knees, turning him weak and weightless. He turned and looked at Jenny, but Jenny looked away. He looked at the stranger again, at the steady, unwavering eyes, then looked down—back up—then off and away—his eyes shifting and blinking—squirming on the inside but paralyzed on the out. He started to speak but his voice ceased up, pinching off. He gulped for another breath... and then another. Then he said, "Well um... where um, where ya goin'?"

"It's time for me to go," said the stranger.

Space started to speak, but again had to stop to clear his throat. "Well uh...you um, you get around here much? I mean, you think, uh, you think you might be back?"

The stranger looked off across the fields to the huge ball of orange setting in the west. "I don't think the man you're waiting for is coming," he said. "I don't think he ever will." He took a breath and let it back out... then looked at Space again. "Another time maybe. Maybe when things are different."

Then the stranger turned and continued on, walking off across the dusty lot...

Space remained frozen, eyes blinking, watching the man walk away, moving off towards the county highway...

Then he yelled out, *"Wait!"*

The stranger stopped and turned.

Space hesitated, then started out across the blowing dusty lot towards the stranger. He stopped directly in front of him, but then looked away. He started to speak, but emotion pinched off his voice again. He looked down and tried to swallow it under; then took a breath, "You uh... you want this?" He held the card out partially towards the stranger. "I mean my dad, um... he uh, he's a hell of a guy and everything, just like I said, but he um, he doesn't really go for the sentimental kinda stuff, so here... here, why don't you take it."

The stranger reached forward and took the card, and Space looked up at him—this time not looking away.

"Thank you," said the stranger. He put his hand on the boy's shoulder and held into his eyes. "Thank you."

Then he turned and walked on, starting up the narrow gravel shoulder of county road 17, walking into the north...

Space remained where he was, not moving, watching the man move further away—the card in hand—his figure slowly fading smaller...

Jenny walked out across the lot to where Space was standing. She put her arm around him, and then turned him away and walked him back towards the building. She led him around the south corner—out of sight of the highway and the stranger—and then sat down with him on a bench that was set out in the grass.

The wind was dying to a breeze by then, stroking the fields gently in soft wrinkles... Jenny leaned closer to Space and held him near. Her eyes looked off towards the sun, watching it lower slowly, settling easily into the land in the west...

Space's eyes stared absently at the fields.

Neither of them moved, neither spoke... while behind them— beyond Pepper-Dines—the stranger continued to shrink smaller, fading further into the distant north... walking all alone up the long, empty highway.

A GOOD PIECE IS HARD TO FIND

It was in the Hard-Tack Saloon, Big Horn, Wyoming. Ellen Ray was at the bar, drunk, staring downward into a mixed drink, contemplating her mistake. Hank Jr. was singing about whiskey and women on the jukebox.

"You okay there darling?" a man's voice said.

The voice was to Ellen Ray's immediate left. She didn't answer. If it wasn't a mistake, why did it feel like one? Where would she be now if she'd never met him? She took another sip and set her glass back on the bar.

"Can I give you a lift or anything?" the man asked. He moved closer to Ellen Ray and slid an arm around her. "What's your name?" he said. Then his hand began a subtle massage along her shoulder.

Ellen Ray did not look up. She didn't move. She just said calmly, "I don't need a lift, and git yer goddamn paw off me."

"*Hey, hey,* come on," said the man. He seemed suddenly surprised, partially retracting his hand. "I just thought maybe you'd had a few too many to be driving, that's all. I just thought I'd, you know, offer you a ride or something."

Ellen Ray lifted her head, not looking at the man. She blinked, then focused her liquor-weighted eyes ahead, staring into the glowing bottles behind the bar...

"I mean a nice looking girl like you shouldn't be sitting alone in a place like this," said the man. "Just thought I could maybe, you know, help you find your way out of here or something. Maybe I could take you someplace a little more... *civilized.* What's your name?"

"Where?"

"Huh?"

Ellen Ray turned to the man and then repeated: "Where?"

"*Oh*—well hey," said the man, "anywhere you say!" He stepped back with a smile and open arms like he was willing to accommodate.

Ellen Ray studied the fellow. He was older than her—by a good twenty years, she figured. Mid-fifties or so, in a business suit.

"Then what?"

"Then what? Well then it's... *hey,* whatever you say!" said the man. He stepped closer again with eyebrows raised.

"Why you wanna give me a ride," said Ellen Ray, "because you're concerned I can't drive, or because you're after somethin' else?"

The man broke into a laugh and ran a hand up over his hair. He tugged at his ear and glanced around the bar. Then he said, "You ah, you certainly are a blunt one, aren't you?"

"Well what is it?"

"Ah, well, gosh, I don't know."

"Whata'ya mean—you '*don't know'?*"

"Well, you know," said the man, and he laughed again, pulling up on his pants. He reached up and pinched his nose, then glanced around the barroom again. "Let's put it this way," he said, "let's just say that I'd like to, ah... be *with you.* How's that?"

"What for?"

"*What for?*"

"Yeah, why not that old gal over there? Why me?"

The man shrugged, leaving his shoulders upwardly suspended.

"Well, maybe I think you're—"

"Drunk and easy?"

The man laughed politely, then said, "No, actually I think you—"

"Have a nice ass?"

"What? *No!*"

"You don't think I have a nice—"

"Well yeah— I mean, *yeah,* but—"

"Have you looked at it?"

"What? Looked at—well, no, not really, but—"

"Then how can you say, '*yeah'?*"

"Well, I can just sort've, you know, I can tell."

Ellen Ray slid off her barstool. "Take a look."

"Pardon?"

"I said, *take a look.* Look it over and tell me what you think."

Ellen Ray stood in front of the man and turned for him, turning around slowly in place...

The man's eyes dropped down over her—lowering over her white western shirt to her firm, slender curves—her thin, delicate waist and tight denim thighs... then back up again to her long sun-streaked hair laying flat against her back—soft and smooth—disheveled finger strokes pushed through the top...

"Well, whata'ya think?"

"Wow," said the man.

"What does that mean?"

"I mean, that's... pretty nice."

"Now let's see yours."

"What?"

"I said, *'let's see* yours'. I showed you mine, so show me yours."

The man chuckled again and reached for his drink.

"C'mon, turn around! Let's see!"

The man retracted his reach and put both hands up in front of himself like he was being arrested. He started to utter something, but then just shrugged and began to turn.

"Hold your suit up, so I can see."

"Whatever you say baby," said the man, and he held it up, turning like Ellen Ray had, except in a hastier manner.

"That kinda sucks."

"What?"

"How much money you got?"

"Money?"

Ellen Ray put a hand on her hip. "Yeah, money."

The man began to squint slightly, then ruffled his brow into a curious frown.

"What—you don't know?"

The man looked both ways, up and down the bar, then leaned in closely towards Ellen Ray. He cleared his throat and in a discreet tone said, "Hey, ah... are you ay uh... you a *professional?*"

Ellen Ray cracked a broad smile and glanced away.

"No, I mean... *Are you?*"

Ellen Ray looked at the man again. "You tellin' me you don't even know who you're talkin' to?"

"Well, I don't know," said the man. The smile had returned to his face, a growing smile, a knowing smile. "Why don't you tell me, who ah, who am I talking to?" He said it like a man who was about to receive a prize.

Ellen Ray's smile disappeared. She moved in towards the man's ear, lowering her voice to a tone that was soft but direct. "You're talkin' to the best piece of girl in the state of Wyoming, boy. *That's* who I am."

The man swallowed deeply and licked his lips.

Ellen Ray stepped back again. "Now, how much you got?"

The man's hand went to his pocket. "I ah—I don't know, I—"

"You got a hundred?"

"A hundred? Yeah."

"You got two?"

"Yeah."

"Three?"

"*Three?* Well, I don'—"

"You gotta understand, it takes money," said Ellen Ray. "I mean you're not exactly what I'd *call great,* you know."

"Oh yeah—no, I know," said the man. He seemed suddenly anxious. "I mean, I don't claim to be Brad Pitt or anything."

"That's good. 'Cause you're not. And actually, it's gonna take everything you've got."

"What, everything I've got—" the man broke out laughing again, then reached up and pinched his nose, same as before. "You're kind of a crazy little thing, aren't you?"

"Crazy?" said Ellen Ray. "Maybe so."

"Look darling, let's put a number on it," said the man. He glanced both directions again, then reached for his drink. "Or, maybe we could go to my room, and we could, you know, discuss it there."

"Discuss it here."

"Look, let's cut through the bullshit okay? I've got plenty to take care of you, so let's get out of here and we'll figure it out, alright?"

"I don't think so," said Ellen Ray. She turned away from the man and sat back up on her stool.

"Hey wait," said the man. He set his drink back on the bar and lowered his tone again. "Okay, so you're a tough negotiator. Look, I ah—I have an extra hundred, okay? How 'bout that? We'll make it *three* then, okay?"

"No," said Ellen Ray.

"*No?* Well, what then? What do you want—four? Alright, four. I'll give you four hundred bucks—but let's just go then, alright?"

"No."

"*No?* Well, now what, what do you want?"

"Forget it."

"Forg—" the man glanced away and pursed his lips. He took a breath and moved closer to Ellen Ray again, lowering his voice even further, "Look," he finally said, "how much do you want?"

"How much do I want?" said Ellen Ray. "I want my life." She looked at the man again. "Can you give me that?"

"I don't know what you mean," said the man. "C'mon, I'll give you five hundred bucks."

"Spend the money on your wife."

"My *wife*—what?" said the man. He picked up his drink and took a quick sip. The Judds were singing from the jukebox by this time, harmonizing sweetly over the barroom.

"Yeah, maybe you're right," said Ellen Ray. "Spend it on your kids."

"Oh Christ," mumbled the man—mostly to himself. Then he set his drink back on the bar.

"You do that," said Ellen Ray, "and I'll appreciate it."

The man let out another huff of a breath and looked off across the barroom. He smiled and shook his head but did not say anything.

Ellen Ray had turned away from the man, resting her elbows back on the bar. She watched the man's figure in the mirror, out the corner of her eye. He remained like a statue, not moving... Then he turned and walked away and was gone.

Ellen Ray pushed her drink ahead, out of the way. She just wanted to sit for a bit, listen to the music and contemplate her thoughts...

... And soon she was thinking of other things again... difficult things, troubled things... things that were good for a short while, a long time ago...

... She could still see him, breaking out of the chute, riding high on that wild animal, his white-bloused upper and pearl-snapped cuffs flailing forwards and backwards and sideways, his narrow belt line centered over the turmoil, his Championship buckle glinting in the sun, and all those thousands *cheering*...

... *Thousands*...

... She could hear him too—his voice—telling her that he could've had *anybody* and that the only reason he *picked her,* was because of her *ass.*

Yeah, that was *him.* He liked to walk around the house like some sort of stud and tell her that the only reason he didn't dump her was because she just happened to have the nicest ass in the state of Wyoming—and then would quickly remind her that that wasn't necessarily saying a whole lot, so she'd better keep her cooking good and keep her housekeeping in order, just to be safe.

It caused Ellen Ray to smile—those thoughts mixed with the whiskey. She didn't know why, because she felt disappointment. A lot of it, mostly in herself. Why had she done it? He was so full of himself, so *cocky.* He didn't even realize his own shortcomings. He was, for the most part, numb to areas where he was so... *lacking.*

Ellen Ray's thoughts slid slowly deeper. Her smile faded and her eyes stared idly downward again at nothing. He had been a star for a short time, for a brief moment—one whose fifteen minutes had come and gone a long time ago. She wanted to go back. Do it over again. Do something different. Would she actually do something different? Take a different path, pick another option? What had she missed? There were so many lives she could have lived, but she had chosen this one. Why? There were so many opportunities she could have taken, but she settled with *him.* Why? Maybe there was still time. She still had some youth on her side. She still had some looks, a pocket-full of smarts and a little bit of wit. She had been given the whole package in life but what had she done with it? What had it gotten her, where had it landed her? *Here.* Right here—in a dusty little western town, where she was sitting on a barstool, medicating herself amongst a bunch of drunken simpletons.

The whole experience had been like a drug that had slowly worn off. She thought of how the drug had changed her—and then changed her again as it wore down. She thought of different times he had disappointed her over the years and she'd criticized him and gotten after him for not measuring up—times she'd put him down for not being what she'd expected him to be, for not being what he was *supposed to be,* for not being what he'd once been when he was riding high and all those thousands were cheering...

... But when she got to the bottom, the very bottom, there was still something good about him. He was honest, at least. And he did have heart. And for a short time, a long while ago, he had actually felt like something... *special...*

... And it was sitting with those thoughts in the Hard-Tack Saloon, that Ellen Ray recalled that feeling. And for a fleeting moment, like a passing breeze that would soon be gone, she felt it again—but only in memory—the same way she had felt it those several years ago on that sunny afternoon in Cheyenne—after the two of them had left all the *cheering thousands* behind, and were alone and close... feeling like the *luckiest girl in the whole USA.*

Ellen Ray sensed another figure in the mirror moving back across the barroom towards her... He sat down on the stool next to hers.

"The kids are asleep," he said. "I told the sitter we'd be back by eleven."

Something was coming over Ellen Ray, rushing up through her, a warm, weightless sensation—maybe it was the whiskey, she didn't know, but she suddenly felt like she was going to cry. She turned to the one next to her and wrapped her arms around him—

'Hey, hey, what the hell," he said, "what's goin' on?" He was surprised, but he put his arms around her and held her in return.

"I love y—," Ellen Ray started to say. She said it into his ear, her voice weak, almost a whisper. Then she tried to say it again... but couldn't.

His arms wrapped tighter, holding her just as they always had, holding her gently, but firm.

And Ellen Ray also tried to wrap tighter, just as she had on that sunny afternoon in Cheyenne, those many years ago... Giving the best she could... with the little she had left.

FINAL DELIVERY

June 1993

It was the third time the Dominos man had been back to the same address; it was also the third time he had received no answer at the door, and the third time the two Mexicans across the street had sat outside their house and laughed. The residence in question looked like a gang house or a drug place. The yard was infested with weeds and filth—with cancerous vegetation, litter, and junk. There were parts of an old stove tipped over into a bush—a rusted sink, a diaper, an old couch wrecked and rotting in the sun. The place stunk.

The Dominos man stood on the broken front steps trying to retain his composure as the laughter and remarks continued across the street behind him. He focused on the door in front of him, on the peeling paint and fungus, then took several deep breaths, as if he were about to enter the starting gate of a grueling athletic competition. Then he turned with the pizza—a large *Extravaganza*—and walked back out to the street towards his pickup—a Chevy half ton with Minnesota plates and a plastic Dominos sign mounted on the roof. He had bought the pickup while in college, in Fargo, and had used it while working construction during the summers. He had then taken it with him when he'd come out west five years ago to write for the movies—a decision his father had told him was *foolish*.

It was beginning to dawn on the Dominos man now—as it had been for some time—that his father may have been right. As he approached his vehicle now, he wondered what might have happened had he listened to his father and stayed in Minnesota. By now, he most certainly would've been a supervisor in his father's company and would probably be living in a house of his very own—probably on a lake—and probably with a wife and kids.

But instead, he had decided to change directions in life. He had decided to take a road of greater risk—to aim for higher goals, loftier ideals—and become a writer. He had chosen to take a gamble—and play the game—go to Hollywood and tell his stories. He had placed all of his marbles on this endeavor and now he had failed—and he had become humiliated in the process. After five years of unwavering commitment, the road of dreams had essentially landed him here, at this specific point, in this particular predicament—in a silly blue and red Dominos smock, carrying a large thermal bag with a toxic *Extravaganza* inside, returning to his pickup which was parked along a derelict street in Burbank California—which he had been summoned to once again by the two taunting thugs from across the street.

Yes, maybe his father had been right. Maybe what he had chosen to do with his life *had* been foolish. It had amounted to five years of frustration, five years of failure. He had been struggling in an industry full of hustlers, fakes, and nepotists—trying to compete with other writers who, unlike himself, brought no *real-life* experience to the table. The other writers hadn't grown up as he had—in a *real town,* up north, in the outdoors—hunting and adventuring, trapping and fishing—doing real things, real work. They didn't understand *real life—real stories*—and the people above them—the agents, producers, and development people—they didn't seem to understand it either. The entire industry was made up of the same people—transient, Hollywood suburbanites who had learned life by watching television and by going to the movies—soulless, pseudo-artistic quacks who had grown up in the safety of their bedrooms, where they had taken refuge from the world by reading books and playing techno games.

The reason these people became writers—or came to Hollywood—was also deficient. It was shallow and misguided. They had come because they merely wanted *to be writers,* not because they had anything significant to say. They came because they wanted to be a part of *Hollywood,* a part of *the movies,* not because they had anything to offer the world, not because they were filled with any great passion to speak some new vision, or to reveal some new found truth.

As the Dominos man stepped off the curb now, one of the Mexicans said something in a belligerent tone—something about *white* about *All-American.* The Mexicans were sitting in the shade in front of their house—or *somebody's* house—near a car that was parked too closely to the front steps. The car looked hostile. It had shiny wheels and dark windows and had hot orange flames painted along the fenders.

The Dominos man continued past his pickup and crossed the street, walking towards the two Mexicans, with the pizza perched against his left shoulder in a classical, delivery-type posture. One of the Mexicans was wearing baggy, sloppy clothing with a flannel shirt tied around his waist, his hair dyed blondish red—which dangled out from under, what looked to be a backwards LA Raiders cap. The other wore sunglasses and an earring, with slicked back hair; a white tank-top undershirt showing off muscles and dull colored tattoos.

"Hey Domino boy, you bringing us a pizza?"

The Dominos man continued towards the two, crossing over the municipal grass and sidewalk, then onto their driveway.

"You guys order this?"

"No, the asshole across the street did man, but he don't fuckin' hear too good. You gotta knock louder."

The Mexican with the LA Raiders cap flicked down a cigarette and stood up. "Hey Domino, let's see what you got in the bag, man."

The Dominos man kept his course, walking directly towards the two until he was within only a few feet. Then he stopped. He stood alongside the hostile car with the orange flames.

"Did you guys order this or not?"

The Mexican with the sunglasses and slicked back hair also got up and started lazily towards him. "What if we fuckin' did, man?"

"Then you pay for it."

The Mexican with the Raiders cap moved to the Dominos man's side. "You gonna take money from us, Domino boy?"

"Hey Domino, you talk pretty fuckin' brave, man. You fuckin' proud?"

"Not really," said the Dominos man, then he pulled out from under his smock a Colt .380 automatic. "How 'bout you?"

The Mexicans stopped. The one with the reddish hair and Raiders cap put up his hands and began backing away. "Hey, hey, fuck man, take it cool."

The one with the slicked back hair and sunglasses put his hands on his hips and lazily stood his ground. "Hey, you got some sort of fuckin' problem, man?"

"I sure do," said the Dominos man: and with that admission, he abided by a creed that he had been taught as a boy—taught to him by his father. A code concerning firearms.

1. Never point a gun at *anything,* unless you intend to shoot.

2. Never shoot, unless you intend to kill.

The Dominos man abided fully, completing the accord with five quick pulls of the trigger. When finished, he stood blinking for a short time, his ears boxed in from the rapid *banging* noise, his heart pounding heavily in his chest. He was disorientated for several seconds, unable to hear, and his balance was somewhat off. He looked next door, to the neighbors house, expecting to see chaos—faces in the windows, people screaming... but there was nothing. He looked to the other side—to the other house—expecting to see people emerging, or stirring, but again, there was nothing. He looked at the two Mexicans. They were laid out on the ground—the one with his hands behind his back as if he were playing *guess which hand,* his shades down on the base of his nose like reading glasses, his eyes staring over them, up at the sun. The one with the blondish red hair was further back, twitching—his leg and foot—and a long hiss was seething out of him, sounding like the life being let out of an air mattress. The Dominos man turned away from it, looking across the street, then looked both ways, up and down the block, expecting hysteria, a gathering crowd, a mob, cops, people looking from windows, rushing out into the street... But again, there was nothing. Nothing odd, nothing unusual. The only person in sight was at the far end of the block, at the cross-street—a jogger passing by with a dog following behind—in view only for a second, and then gone.

The Dominos man waited. He listened for sirens. Surely there would be sirens—and helicopters too—there were always sirens and helicopters. But the only noticeable sound was the *quiet.* He'd never heard Burbank so quiet...

There was some low thumping music somewhere, coming from down the street—an approaching car, a brightly polished machine with flashing dingo lights and smoke black windows. The car passed by without looking—kids—then faded down the block and disappeared.

The Dominos man walked back out to the street, still holding the warm pizza against his shoulder and the warm Colt along his side. He looked up and down the block again, then tucked the Colt back under his smock and crossed the street to his pickup, his eyes scanning the houses, up and down, looking for *somebody—anybody—*an old woman peering out from behind a curtain, perhaps...

But again, there was nothing.

The Dominos man got into his pickup and set the pizza on the passenger side, then started the vehicle and let it idle for a minute. He thought about the pizza—considering for a moment what he should do with it. He considered the normal routine: return to Dominos with it and report it as a *no-show*. Then he considered keeping it for himself—but immediately rejected the idea. Then he considered throwing it into a dumpster and paying for it himself, and saying nothing to anybody about any of it until he was asked.

He chose the latter.

Then he quit his job.

After which, he went home to his studio apartment, sat in his Director's chair and waited. He did not turn on any lights, or turn on the television. He did not turn on his radio. In the distance he could hear the sounds of sirens and helicopters—which he thought surely would be coming soon, coming to arrest him, and to take him away. He had expected them to show up at Dominos—when he had turned in his smock and hat, and the plastic sign off the top of his pickup; but again there had been nothing.

As the Dominos man sat waiting, he scanned his studio apartment, staring at the tangibles that remained in his life—all collected before him now in one room. There was the card table with his word processor on top, his notes, and his Colt .380 automatic. There was the final draft of his latest screenplay, *A Brush With Fire*— a story about two guys smuggling Indian artifacts out of Canada, through the woods of Northern Minnesota—a great tale about smugglers, Indians, and FBI agents—which he had been told needed a rewrite—that it was too dark, not commercial, not marketable. On the floor was his mattress, and against the wall—on blocks and planks— were his books and plants and a few remaining personal items.

As evening came, his apartment slipped into silhouette, then into darkness, and when morning arrived he went for a walk.

Upon his return, he expected to be greeted by flashing lights and sirens; but again, there was nothing. He even stood outside his door—on the stairs—and listened for a minute... But the only sounds were of an argument next door—a neighbor slapping his girlfriend or wife, the woman screaming profanities in retaliation. A baby was crying somewhere, and there was a helicopter off in the distance, but nothing out of the ordinary.

During the next several days, the Dominos man remained mostly in his apartment. He did not turn on any lights or turn on the television. He did not turn on his radio or plug in the phone. He did not buy a newspaper or even look at one. He talked to nobody.

On the third day, maybe the fourth, he began to sing. He sang only one song and sang it repetitively. It was an old Elton John tune that he knew from high school called, *Goodbye Yellow Brick Road.* He stuck mostly to the same verse, and especially to one line—

I should've stayed on the farm
I should've listened to my old man...

He sang quietly at first, internally—almost in a

whimper—like a patient in a home for the mentally unbalanced. Then his voice began to evolve, gradually becoming louder and more passionate, then expanding into other verses—and soon he was singing like Elton himself, standing in front of the bathroom mirror, pouring all his soul into the barrel of his .380 Colt.

From the bathroom he went to his window, an upper level perch that over-looked the rooftops of Burbank, where he sang to the periodic sounds of sirens and helicopters, singing out to them with open arms, as if welcoming them upon their late arrival.

> I'm not a present for your friends to open
> this boy's too young to be singin'
> the blue-oo-oo-oos
> ah-h-h-h-h-h
> ah-h-h-h-h.

He then stripped himself naked and grabbed an Indian belt off the wall that usually hung as decor, and strapped it thinly around his waist. He lay down in the middle of his apartment, lying spread eagled on his back on the dirty brown carpet and stared up at the smog-soiled plaster and continued to sing, singing with introspection again, singing with depth—

> You can't plant me in your penthouse
> I'm goin' back to my plow—

He later added a pair of socks to his attire which he pretended were boots, then changed voices again and moved back to his Director's chair. He sat with his legs crossed, a glass of LA tap water in hand, and began taking a very intellectual approach to the composition. The belt that he wore had been purchased on Melrose Avenue, from an Indian named *Light Spirit,* who told him that the colorful beads were *mystical* and that the belt would keep him *spiritually centered,* keep him balanced—and that it was a one of a kind deal for $135.00.

With his newly assumed position, the Dominos man began searching for additional depth in the piece—for further meaning— occasionally interspersing it with an emotionally charged segment which included rising up and prancing across to the window, where again he would sing to the sirens and helicopters—belting out a couple of verses especially for them—

> Maybe you'll get a replacement
> there's plenty like me to be found
> mongrels, who ain't got a penny
> sniffin' for tears just like you
> on the *ground*
> ah-h-h-h-h-h-
> ah-h-h-
> So goodbye yellow brick road...

That last part he started to love. He reassumed his spread eagled position on the floor again, and began doing harmony on that last part with Nigel Olsson. Nigel Olsson was cool. The Dominos man remembered the first time he'd seen him—on the back of the Honky Chateau album or Greatest Hits album or one of those. Everybody thought he was a girl. He looked just like one—the way he was sitting there with that long black hair and those Indian fringed pants. Then it turned out that he was a guy, so next, everyone thought he was an Indian, a Cherokee or something. Then everybody found out that he was just exactly what he was supposed to be—just a very cool British drummer in Elton John's band.

The Dominos man couldn't stop thinking about Nigel Olsson. He hated the thought, but he remembered having sexual thoughts about Nigel Olsson when he was in about ninth grade—when he still thought Olsson was a girl.

Now he wondered what Nigel Olsson looked like naked. As he lay there on his back, spread eagled on the floor, he wondered what it would be like to have Nigel Olsson in his apartment with him, lying next to him on the carpet, lying naked with him. . . touching him.

When the next morning came, those same thoughts from the previous evening made the Dominos man want to throw up. He tried to induce vomiting by sticking a finger down his throat, but it didn't work, it only gagged him. He felt sick. He felt empty and weightless... .

This was on the seventh day, and it was on this day that he stopped singing. On the ninth day he got dressed. And on the eleventh he left LA.

He bundled his belongings into a tarp in the back of his pickup, then took the 10 freeway east to the 15, and then followed it north to Las Vegas, where he pulled off and cruised the strip, going past the Flamingo, past Caesars and the Mirage, looking at all the people—at all the losers from all parts of the country, and at all the girls. *Girls.* He suddenly wanted to see one naked. He wanted to see one up close, so he kept cruising, watching for signs that said, GIRLS. He eventually wound up on the other side of the freeway, at a dirty little low slung place that looked like a roadside store on one of the Indian Reservations back in Minnesota, except this place had a flashing sign on top—pink and green—that said: TIPS & TOTS—*NUDE DANCERS*.

The Dominos man went inside and started to drink. The place was scattered with old men in cheap suits and toupees, and a few younger guys who looked like they worked in science labs—and one guy who was right out of a time warp, right out of *Saturday Night Fever*—John Travolta with the white suit, gold chains, and poofed-up hair.

The first few Dancers were a little rough, but after a few beers they got pretty good. The Dominos man walked over to John Travolta and asked him if he knew who he looked like, and Travolta ignored him. The Dominos man sat down at Travolta's table and Travolta *said* something rude, in a New York accent that sounded to the Dominos man like some sort of gangster talk. They both sat together at the table and drank and watched the show, and then Travolta asked the Dominos man what he did for a living, and the Dominos man told Travolta that he was a screenwriter, and that he was under contract with United Artists in LA.

Travolta suddenly became friendly. He told the Dominos man that he produced movies. He told him that he was looking for new scripts, and that he would like to hire a new writer; on spec.

The Dominos man had suddenly had enough of Travolta. He left Travolta's table and went over and talked to one of the toupee men—who told him that he was the guy who had invented *in-flight refueling* for jets, and that he had a new invention that was going public— Fortune 500 or something—and that he was looking for a new partner. Then the most beautiful girl that the Dominos man had ever seen in his entire life came out on stage. She was stunning. She was young and gorgeous, and was a good dancer too, and her body was nearly perfect. Some of the old men in toupees and a couple of the scientists reached up and tucked dollar bills in through the dancer's G-string— the refueling man amongst them, giving her a buck. The Dominos man dug into his money and counted it, while Travolta sat down at his table and smoked a cigarette. The Dominos man did some adding and subtracting, figuring out how much money he would need for the remainder of his trip, then he staggered up to the edge of the stage and started sticking money into the girl's G-string—one hundred dollars' worth—in crumpled twenties, tens, and fives, shouting up to her over the music, telling her that she was amazingly talented and that she should never give up her dream, because she was going to be a star. The starlet smiled at the Dominos man while dancing in place. She pushed *her* hair back and flicked it, mouthing the words *thank you* to him several times.

Soon after that the Dominos man left. He started up his pickup and got back onto I-15 and when daylight came he was in northern Utah. When he finally sobered up, he was in Wyoming, and when he got out into the middle of the state and was cruising at a steady eighty-five miles per hour, he began to feel hungry. He couldn't remember when the last time was he had eaten. He had no money for food—only for gas—and now he was beginning to regret giving the last of his money to the dancer. He became frustrated and wanted to rebel. He wanted to strike at something, but *at what*—or how—he didn't know. The day was hot and dry and there was nobody in sight, just himself and the big sky, and an endless scape of barren planet. He thought about his Colt .380 on the seat alongside him, thought about it down inside the canvas bag. He thought about putting it to his head and pulling the trigger while doing 85 miles per hour—and the thought of this made him smile for a moment. He liked the idea and wondered if anybody had ever tried it before—wondered what the whole scene would look like, what the crash would be like. He suddenly reached over and dug down into the bag, and pulled out a small cardboard box—a Maxell floppy disc box—with a piece of sticker paper across the front that said, *A Brush With Fire.* He threw the box and its contents out the window, then reached into the bag again and rummaged around some more, pulling out the final draft of *A Brush With Fire.* He laid the manuscript on his lap and pulled out the brass clasps from Charlie Chans copy shop, then threw the manuscript out the window, watching it explode in his side mirror — blowing into a turbulent puff of white—a hundred and twenty-two sheets to the wind. Gone. Next he reached down and unbuckled his $135.00 mystic Indian belt that he'd purchased from *Light Spirit* on Melrose Avenue, jerked it out of his waist loops and threw *it* out too.

Then he took several deep breaths and put both hands on the wheel. He focused on the highway.

He followed it further east and further north, backtracking the same path he had taken five years earlier, retracing his way back on the *Yellow Brick Road.* He was tired and hungry but he ignored it. He stopped only for gas and he spoke to no one. As trees began to reappear, and the terrain around him became slowly familiar, five years of life began to drop off behind—quickly becoming distant—as if a great gravitational pull was lapsing it off into memory. He suddenly felt aware of everything around him—of clean air, of color, of sounds— of the *humming* of the motor and of the wind whistling up near the tops of the windows. He switched on the radio and there was a song playing that he hadn't heard in years—*Sister Golden Hair*. He had never really cared much for the tune—it reminded him of getting ready for school in twelfth grade—but right now, for some reason, it sounded pretty good. He listened to the music with an odd pleasure and even started to hum with it. Then he began to sing, . .

His focus however remained on the road.

The *Yellow Brick Road...*

... Which he would follow back to his beginnings—back to his place in the woods—where he would pick up where he had left off, and allow the dreams of his youth to slowly fade, to disappear into the past, until one day any recollection of what had happened would no longer linger, no longer exist, but would slip off into darkness, and become forever... gone.

ABOUT ATMOSPHERE PRESS

Atmosphere Press is an independent, full-service publisher for excellent books in all genres and for all audiences. Learn more about what we do at atmospherepress.com.

We encourage you to check out some of Atmosphere's latest releases, which are available at Amazon.com and via order from your local bookstore:

Home is Not This Body, a novel by Karahn Washington

Whose Mary Kate, a novel by Jane Laclere Doyle

Stuck and Drunk in Shadyside, a novel by M. Byerly

These Things Happen, a novel by Chris Caldwell

Vanity: Murder in the Name of Sin, a novel by Rhiannon Garrard

Blood of the True Believer, a novel by Brandann R. Hill-Mann

The Dark Secrets of Barth and Williams College: A Comedy in Two Semesters, a novel by Glen Weissenberger

The Glorious Between, a novel by Doug Reid

An Expectation of Plenty, a novel by Thomas Bazar

Sink or Swim, Brooklyn, a novel by Ron Kemper

Lost and Found, a novel by Kevin Gardner

Eaten Alive, a novel by Tim Galati

The Sacrifice Zone, a novel by Roger S. Gottlieb

Olive, a novel by Barbara Braendlein

ABOUT THE AUTHOR

Initially a playwright, Mark Thorson's writing career launched when his first play, *To Cheat A Clown*, was produced at the Pan Andreas Theater in Los Angeles, which soon shifted into a career of writing screenplays, two of which were sold under option, which paid his Hollywood rent for several years.

His writing gradually evolved into prose which allowed him to return to his roots in northern Minnesota, where he also became a successful businessman, presiding over the highway construction company, Mark Sand & Gravel Co.

Thorson now lives in northern Minnesota and southern California, where he is currently at work on the novel, *American Ice,* a story that includes characters from three of the stories in *Final Delivery* — *The Fifty Dollar Assassin, A Trip Back Down* and *The Gift.*

Thorson's formal education includes both the arts and commerce. He is an alumnus of both the American Film Institute in Los Angeles, as well as the Harvard Business School in Boston.

CPSIA information can be obtained
at www.ICGtesting.com
Printed in the USA
FSHW010205080721
82910FS

9 781636 495804